Passenger

Passenger
Copyright 2016 by LM Pampuro

Cover design by the LMPatarini group

ISBN: 978-1-7344990-2-5

Passenger

LM Pampuro

Passenger

L.M. Pampuro

LM Pampuro

This is dedicated to my fellow travelers
who have danced under the stars,
tried to capture the magic on tape,
and have ventured out of their comfort zones
to experience the bliss.

LM Pampuro

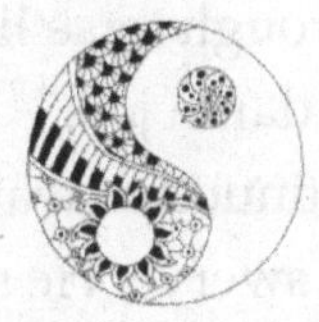

"Is that her?"

"Yeah." Weston Traynor stood still. His dark brown eyes fixated on the figure, moving in front of him. He watched her bright-colored clothing swirl in between the pine trees. Her long peasant skirt billowed out then hugged tight against her small body as she took turns spinning in each direction. Vivid rainbow colors exploded in between the large dark brown trunks like fireworks bursting across the sky. He tucked the binoculars back into the case hanging around his neck, yet his gaze never left her. "Crap," he muttered under his breath as he scratched his forehead.

"She's cute," Conrad Beman observed. Conrad turned back toward his direct supervisor and waited for a response. He had only worked with Weston for six months and had already picked up on his boss' quirks, one of which was being alone with his thoughts. Against his better judgment, Conrad teased, "Whatcha going to do boss?"

"My job," Weston answered without hesitation. His biceps tightened, and he turned to glare at Beman. Through terse lips, he repeated, "I am going to do my damn job."

Weston continued to watch the radiant silhouette spin and swerve. He stood close enough to catch the nuances of her body, yet far enough away so she didn't find his observations, not that she would notice anyway.

A static buzz in his earpiece interrupted his thoughts.

"Go ahead," Weston replied in a low tone.

"The driver is hanging out with people taping the show, just like last time," both Weston and Beman heard through the white noise. "I could bring him in for marijuana possession because that is all I have seen him do."

Weston looked at the ground and shook his head. "Where is the other male passenger?" he questioned through gritted teeth. "Is he with the driver?" It amazed him how often the intelligent people around him seemed to miss the big picture.

"I don't see him, boss. He was here at the start, but once the music began, you know, people stood up to dance..."

Weston took in a deep breath. He glanced over at Beman. *Was he laughing?* With a clear voice, Weston enunciated each word, almost as if addressing a child, "Please do not apprehend for marijuana. Try to find the other male and…" Weston looked over at the figure in the trees, "observe at close range but do not apprehend."

Beman added, "Get photos of the transactions." Weston glared over but relaxed at Beman's shrug.

"Out," Weston barked. "Some people just don't get what we're trying to accomplish here."

"Yeah – it's the old windshield bug thing, boss." Weston nodded and smiled, yet he looked confused. "You know, like…"

"It is ok, Beman. I'm good." He turned back to the girl.

Tonight Weston stayed to see the magic of her movements. He watched other concertgoers stop to stare. When she didn't reciprocate their attention, they would skip off toward the sound. Some tried to dance with her. Some offered a hit of marijuana or a sip of soda. She would smile and decline with a simple nod, oblivious to all the fuss. As long as the music played, she just spun in circles. Her arms swayed up to the moonlight then fell wrapping around her slim body. When the music stopped, she picked up her backpack, which was never out of reach.

While his boss keeps an eye on the subject, Conrad started packing up the binoculars, microphones, and other surveillance equipment. Weston held out his hand, and Conrad placed the

Nikon digital in it without needing to ask. They, too, were doing a dance both had completed many times in a short time.

Weston brought the camera to his eye and focused the lens. Soft clicking sounds filled the air. The figure moved in slow motion inside the scope of his lens. He brought the camera down to check out his work. His lips formed a grin. In between her long brown hair, he caught a glimpse of a smile, not a full-blown, laughing, having the time of her life, smile. This was just a soft, serene, Mona Lisa upturn of her lips. She knew something. It was a secret that she wasn't going to share with the world. It was a secret she kept close to her heart.

He shook his head to clear her image and sighed. "We are done here." Weston took one last look at the figure in the trees then headed towards the gate.

"Ok, boss," Conrad replied. He grabbed the two cases off the ground and then caught up to follow Weston back through the pine trees and into the darkness. "What's next?"

"If the pattern continues, the next stop is home for us," Weston gave a tired smile. "We've come this far. Might as well put a tail on their car and see where they go."

"Do you have any idea where they'll head?"

"Eventually they'll be in DC, the next stop for the band is somewhere in Pennsylvania. I'll have the team follow the car best they can and pick up the stragglers left along the way. You and I," Weston hesitated to label their relationship, "are flying home. We will get reports from the road."

"Boss, do you really think she's involved?" Beman held a branch so both could walk by. A single light lit the parking lot, leaving most of it in the quiet darkness.

"I would like to think that bad luck brought her to the wrong place at the wrong time, but I really don't know." He popped open the trunk and rearranged the equipment to fit in perfect form. "We'll find out either way."

"So, in theory, we are down to finding the distribution list and then…"

"Let us not get ahead of ourselves. We got a way to go yet, but yes, the list would be a tremendous help." Weston slid in the driver's seat and started the car. He took one last glance toward the music, then turned the wheel to the exit and headed out onto the highway.

*****

As the musical notes engulfed her senses, Rina swirled through the trees. She loved the smell of the pine needles mixing in with her patchouli and the occasion sweet whiff of marijuana. Here she is in her world: a world of nature and music.

Now and then, piercing stares from passersby jolted her back to reality. She acknowledged the person with a smile or a nod and checked her backpack as she spun. She used to be more trusting, leaving her belongings by a tree or under a bench or when her traveling buddies had room in the taper's section. That ended in Richmond a few years back when someone stole her bag. Her spidey sense had told her to go get the bag, yet she didn't listen because she wanted to trust her fellow humans. She had left it just three feet away from where she danced. Besides holding all of her clothes for the trip, she had asthma issues, and her inhaler was gone too.

Now she paid attention to her gut, and lately, her traveling buddies had been more on edge. There was to be no extra stuff left in the taper's section. God forbid she wandered back to the car too late after the show, or "Princess Rina, we await your company," would become their go-to phrase. On top of that, Doc had picked up a straggler a few states back, and this new person gave her the creeps. Between his lack thereof hygiene, and the fact the asshole seemed to dictate every move from hotels to eateries, this scrawny, unkempt, stranger just made her stomach turn. Tomorrow is the band's day off, and instead of going home, Rina is going into the city instead of stopping home. Doc hadn't even given her a choice, "I'll drop you at the train station, and then you meet up with us in DC." That just got her goat. She had been his traveling companion for a lot longer than the Asshole—as she had taken to calling him—but now dropped like a strung-out straggler.

Rina opened her eyes and looked up at Jerry playing the guitar on the jumbo screen. A chill traveled all the way up her back, and when she jumped around to look, no one was close by. "Oh well, just my imagination," she concluded while she rubbed to get the warmth back in her arms and shoulders.

The crowd cheered as the band went into a slow version of the classic "CC Rider." Rina started to dance but stopped. Something bothered her. The remaining chill grew stronger. "This is what I get for traveling with assholes," she exclaimed as she brought her backpack to her shoulder. Shivering, Rina took one last glance and skipped back into the crowd

"Rina, stay in the car," Doc instructed. "We'll be right back."

"Yes, sir," Rina mock saluted. Sitting back across the tan leather bench seat, she watched Doc and the Asshole walk around the back of a two-story residential building. A few minutes later, the pair climbed the front steps to the second floor. Movement in the large picture window caught her eye. "Wherever we go, someone's always watching," she said to no one.

Rina was still getting used to the new car smell. Doc had just picked this BMW off the lot before they left for Saratoga. Most of the time, Rina loved traveling with Doc. They were just friends, so there wasn't any expectation, at least not on her end. Besides that, they meshed well. Where she tended to be a bit high strung, Doc was mellow and easy to be around, keeping her stress levels in check. Doc played the part of the over-protective big brother she lacked in real life. He made sure they got to where they were going safe and sound. She needed more people like Doc and fewer assholes in her life. Well, at least one less asshole would make a world of difference.

She peaked out the window, down the oak-lined street. The neighborhood was mature. Beautiful houses built during the turn of the century. From what she could see, each had a grand porch out front along with a driveway leading to a two-car garage in the rear. The brick building where Doc parked had to be the sore point of the community. The metal railings attached to cement balconies were usually attributed to motels more than homes. How was this zoning glitch allowed to happen?

Another mystery stop made directed by the Asshole. Not for the first time, she stared at the ceiling and wondered why Doc gave this idiot full rein with their travel plans. She should be wandering around a parking lot or enjoying an air-conditioned hotel room right now. Instead, she sat outside another random building. At least this was the second stop of the day. At the first stop, Doc stayed in the car with her while the Asshole ran into what looked like a crack house, adorned with broken windows and boarded up doors. Rina could only imagine what the inside looked like.

Then they had to wait while the Asshole fiddled with something in the trunk. This time both Doc and the Asshole got out, and Rina got her orders. "Stay in the car," she mimicked Doc in a whiney voice. She tapped her foot against the opposite door a few times then swiveled her butt around to open the back door. Doc's voice echoed at the same time she slid out of the car to stand with her back against the side panel.

Rina raised her hands up over her head, stood on her tippy toes, and reached for the sky. Then she bent forward and hung as her body folded in half. She positioned herself so that her butt leaned up against the car, and she couldn't be seen from the window. The last thing she needed was a lecture before the next show. The only sound she heard was the "shush" intake of her own breath. No lawnmowers. No birds. No wind.

Last night in Hershey, the band had played a killer show. The stage was set in the middle of the amusement park with the Super Duper Looper coaster hanging in the background. Every few minutes, the rumble of the coaster, followed by screams, would drown out the sounds of the music. Between noises, Rina danced the night away. Today her dancing and traveling with idiots left her with a slight headache. The mystery stops made her stomach nauseous and her patience thin, but nothing would keep her from attending tonight's show. Just like this stop, it was all a minor inconvenience. She would get over it by the time they checked into the Marriott or when the first chords of Jerry's guitar floated through the building. Room service, a hot shower, and a blazing show did so much for her disposition.

That is if they made it to the hotel before the show. Rina sighed as the drapes moved to one side of the slider off the deck. The curious side of her brain wanted to pull her up the stairs to tell the idiots to hurry up. The practical gut side said no way Jose and left her glued to the front of the car.

##

Weston Traynor watched in the distance. The black BMW pulled close to the curb, then two males got out. He observed the driver talking to someone still in the vehicle.

"Can we get audio on the conversation?" he asked. His gaze did not move.

"Yeah. The driver is telling the girl to stay in the car. They'll be right back." Wes nodded. "I got twenty bucks she is out of the car before they get to the meeting."

"I'll take that action," Agent Wilson called from behind.

Weston laughed. "Yeah, she won't listen," he mumbled. "She never did."

"Okay, boss, we got a visual on the apartment. Can't tell who, but someone is watching from behind the drapes."

Weston gazed up at the second-floor apartment. The curtain was positioned open with a slight space between the sliders. He focused in to see a hand creating a peephole. Weston put down his binoculars and looked around the van.

He had put together this team from scratch, being very selective, choosing each man involved. All were military trained, and all were the best at what they did. But since one man went rogue on him, during his first years of doing drug trafficking, he would never again give that level of trust anyone. Although he was proud of the men in front of him, each team member only knew their part in the mission, a trick he had learned during his time in Iraq. Really, only Weston, his department head, and a friend over in internal affairs had the complete details.

"Beman, you are in charge of team one," he instructed. "Wait for my signal then, go. There should be enough evidence to at least hold these guys for a while. Remember we want the big fish. If he sneaks out during the commotion, all this is for nada."

"What about the girl?"

"If she listens and stays in the car," that comment got a snort, "then she gets hauled in with the rest of them…"

"And if she doesn't?"

"I'll cross that bridge…"

"Yo boss, you are crossing," Beman pointed to the slim figure bending over next to the car. "Nice," he sighed. Weston's glare snapped him back. "What do you want us to do?" His chin pointed towards his boss.

Weston tossed his jacket in the car and peeled off his military-issued polo. Underneath his shirt, he wore a white t-shirt from a charity race last spring. He dropped his pants to the floor to reveal runners' shorts.

"I guess you planned ahead?" Beman quipped.

"Something like that," Weston tossed the rest of his clothes in the back. "Someone move my car on the other side. I'll try to distract her to leave the area." For a nanosecond, no one moved until Agent Marcus stepped forward and took his keys.

"You sure…" Beman started to ask.

"Never been more unsure in my life. Our information indicates she may be a valuable asset in taking down Jacko and his entire ring." Weston looked around the room at his team. "If I can't convince her to provide us with information, then I want you to arrest her too."

##

A shadow moved across Rina's feet. She raised her torso to a standing position in time to catch a lone jogger on the opposite side of the street. He looked very ordinary, fitting right in with the neighborhood: short brown hair, beautiful body, sunglasses. The silence bothered her. One hand rubbed her stomach while she wondered where the shadow had come from. She looked around and then just back in time to see the figure cross to her side of the street.

When he got closer, she gave him the tough girl head nod. He replied back with a soft smile then stopped mid-stride.

"Rina?" He reversed toward her. Rina watched his movements, yet when he lifted his sunglasses, she smiled.

"Wes?" She exhaled as she was gripped into a tight and familiar hug. Wes' body felt more muscular than she remembered, but with his arms tight around her, that familiar zing went from her toes to her hair. With a quick shake of her head, a picture of a young couple walking on the beach flashed into her view. The last time the zing happened to her.

"Holy crap! What are you doing here?"

"You need to get out of here," he whispered hard in her ear. Rina pulled back and opened her mouth. As fast as she created the space, Wes brought his lips to hers. He kissed hard and fast. Rina's eyes popped open, but her body softened against his touch. The street, Doc, the band, her backpack, and everything in it disappeared. Her mind flashed back to their junior prom when she and Wes had gotten scolded on the dance floor. Some bad eighties music played in the background as Mrs. Archer lectured about public displays of affection.

Wes pushed her back and caught his ragged breath. "Listen, Rina," he said while pulling her away from the car. "Please come with me. You need to leave."

"Why?" she asked. Rina disengaged her arm from his fingers and folded both arms across her chest. Wes gave her a glare that sent a jolt from her toes to her heart. She glanced back over his shoulder. "I asked you a question," she stated.

Weston hesitated. He couldn't tell her the truth, at least not yet. "I guess 'because I said so' isn't going to work here." Rina acknowledged his comment with a blank stare. "Could you just trust me?" he begged.

"I could, but the last time I trusted you..." Her face flushed. That time she lost something that she could never get back.

Wes looked up at the sliders on the deck, expecting to see the curtain move, but it remained still. "Ok, Rina, here it is. You know what I do for a living," she stared at the ground while she pondered that. "So you know in your gut that if I say you need to leave…" Rina refolded her arms across her chest and thought for a moment about Weston Traynor, the FBI drug agent versus Wes, her ex-boyfriend. Her stomach constricted as she glanced up at the brick building then back at Weston. Why did Doc insist on traveling with assholes?

"Oh what the hell," Rina threw her arms up in the air before adding, "I need to leave a note. Doc gets pissed when I disappear." After she did that once last summer in Oxford, Maine, she was still hearing about how he spent hours searching for her. Though she explained again and again that the fireworks freaked her out, Doc didn't want to listen to it. He just wanted to know she was safe so he could hang out and party instead of combing the lots to look for her.

Rina rounded the car, reached through the open window, and grabbed the blue backpack decorated with dancing bears and buttons. She handed it to Weston, then folded into the driver's side window. The trunk popped open, and Wes diverted his eyes from Rina's body to the building, to the items in the trunk. All appeared to be standard luggage, except a government-issued briefcase with a combination lock. He didn't hide his surprise too well as without thinking, he reached into the trunk to grab the case. As the curtains swayed in the background, he withdrew his hand, reminding himself that he would get to do a more thorough check of the contents once the car was towed back to headquarters.

Rina looked back up to the building in time to catch the curtains sway open then snap closed. "Which one is yours?" Weston inquired.

"Purple roadie case." He came back around with the backpack on his shoulder. His right hand gripped the case. With a head nod, Rina walked to his side. "Hey Wes, the curtain up there..."

Weston grabbed her hand before she could point, "keep moving." He held tight, steering her body behind the car.

"Shit," Weston muttered with a glance back. "Go now," he barked into his shoulder as he pulled Rina toward the corner.

"Any drugs in here?" he barked as he yanked her out of view.

"I don't do any of that crap," Rina answered. She shook her arm free from Weston's grasp then followed him down the street with her arms folded across her chest. Once they turned the corner, out of sight, she stopped.

"Care to explain?" she asked again. Her foot tapped a rhythm against the sidewalk.

Weston moved toward a black sedan. He popped the trunk, tossing the backpack and case inside. Rina stood tight about half a block away. "I forgot to leave a note," she said as she turned in the direction they had just come from. "Doc gets pissed when I randomly disappear."

"Don't worry about Jacko," Weston barked back. "Your note won't do him much good."

"Who's Jacko? Doc's real name is Bruce." Rina's hand started to rub her flipping stomach.

"Jacko is the largest distributor of crystal meth on the east coast. We followed him here from the city." Weston ran his hands over his face. "You people sure travel a lot."

"You people?" Rina turned to face him. "Us people happen to be on the summer tour. Kind of like a traveling vacation, only we see go concerts along the way instead of parking our asses at the beach for a week." Rina pressed her palm into her lower abdomen. "Speaking of which, I need to make sure I have my tickets."

Weston sighed, got out, and brought her bag to her from the trunk. He watched as Rina opened the front pocket to pull out a notebook along with two concert passes, and a plane ticket. He looked out of the corner of his eye, but couldn't tell if there was anything else there.

Rina released a deep breath. "Doc sometimes locks everything in the glove compartment. If he did, we would have to go back." She tucked everything back in its place.

"And what do you mean meth distributor?" she added. "That is so, not Doc."

Weston wondered when she would get back to that. He smiled as he remembered back to when they dated. He would bring up a subject that she would ignore. When he thought she had utterly dismissed it—hours or even days later—Rina would reintroduce their discussion with the addition of her take on the matter. Weston had hoped that her mind would get back to the subject at hand just as quick as it had.

"I have been traveling with Doc for years. He may smoke a little weed. Maybe sells a joint or two on the side. But do anything harder than that? No way. He hates that stuff—lost a life-long friend to an overdose."

"Help me out here, which one is Doc, the driver or the other one?"

"The driver. I don't know the other guy. Doc knows him through someone else. I'm not sure how that all works, but I think we were just giving him a lift as far as DC. At least I hope so."

"The other guy goes by the name Jacko…"

"Jacko? Really?" Rina shook her head. "Well, for the record, I have been calling him the Asshole."

"Good nickname. Have you said it to his face?" Rina let out a nervous laugh. Truth be told, there was something about her traveling partner that made her anxious. She couldn't put her finger on it, yet her stomach never lied. It was the main reason she would lock herself in the hotel bathroom to sleep at night.

Weston turned the key. "He's not a nice guy, Rina. Your friend probably knows that, or you would have been in that house while they were doing their deal."

"Deal? Is that why we've been stopping?" Her eyes got big.

"Pretty much. Only this time, one of the guys in there is a federal agent. Your traveling buddies are about to get busted for distribution of an illegal substance plus a plethora of other charges."

Rina stared ahead, mouth agape. She turned to say something, stopped, shook her head, and then gestured like she was having a silent conversation. When her hand went up, she opened her mouth to start talking, and instead dropped her hand into her lap and shut her mouth. Then the entire routine repeated through.

"But—"

"I saw you in the city," and at the last two concerts, you attended. "Of course, I recognized you immediately. There are some things a guy doesn't forget." Weston took Rina's hand in his and squeezed. Her face turned a bright hue of red. "After I checked you out," she turned toward him and shook his hand free from his touch, "to make sure you were not involved," he added. "I got permission to pull you if the opportunity arose."

"How did the opportunity arise?" Rina asked.

Weston chuckled. "Let's just say it is good to know you still have listening issues." Rina stared back. "Doc told you to stay in the car. If you had listened, I wouldn't have had an opening, but you being you," he laughed, "you had to stretch, and since you got out of the car…"

"So, I created that opportunity?"

"Yeah that 'opportunity.'"

"What does this all mean?" Rina shook her head, "I'm worried about Doc." Her arms hugged her stomach tighter.

"Doc ain't who you think he is."

"I have known Doc for years. I always thought he was a hard-working guy who liked to travel to the occasional concert and blow off steam."

"Yeah—you really don't have a clue, do you?"

"In this instance, I have more of a clue than you do."

"Rina, there is more to all of this than you can see." Weston moved his hand across the dashboard.

"Okay. Let's pretend I don't understand," Rina looked out at another oak-lined street. The mature trees created a canopy over the road. She took in a deep breath and waited for Weston to respond.

"Tangy…"

"No one calls me that anymore."

"Yeah, but I'm not just anyone," Weston reached over and took her hand in his. "Doc really isn't who you think he is."

"You are repeating yourself. You know that circle talk thing drives me nuts. Say what you mean!" Rina inhaled loud. "Look, Wes, I really have known Doc for years, and he pretty much is who he says he is. You know a really nice guy from Massachusetts…" She shook her hand in a feeble attempt to disengage it from Weston's grip. Rina wondered how her hand kept ending up attached to his. "I met him through a mutual friend. One of the straightest guys I know! They were college roommates at the University of Ha…"

"Let's just say that Doc has created quite the illusion for himself," he choked back laughter. "What he did was actually pretty amazing."

"How so?" Weston watched her tongue wet her lips, and then he decided it would be better if he focused on his driving. He turned his gaze back toward the road.

"It just is," Weston smiled. Not satisfied with his answer again, Rina pried her fingers away and folded her hands on her lap.

"Okay, what do you want to know?" Weston shook his head.

"Who do you think Doc is?"

"Doc er, Jacko is a guy from Portland, Maine…"

"Wrong. He is from Massachusetts. Born and raised. You have the wrong person." Rina mimicked a referee gesturing for a touchdown.

"He may live there now…"

"Nope. Met his parents. Actually, I met his whole family. You are getting Doc and the Asshole all mixed up."

"So tell me about the Asshole."

"Don't know much about him, just that I get the sleazy vibe, so when we share hotel rooms, I lock myself in the bathroom and sleep in the tub. I mean ewe… the guy is a creeper, and we have to make a lot of stops for him."

"What kind of stops?"

"You know random places. Sometimes Doc gets out too, but mostly he sits in the car and waits with me."

"You ever go in?"

"Nope. I am told to wait in the car…" Weston burst out laughing, and Rina added,

"Which I usually do because the stops are not in the nicest places, if you know what I mean."

"Really? You don't say."

"Yeah. And the one time I was invited in, I decided to stay in the car and sleep because it was like three in the morning. I think we were in a park somewhere. They kept calling the place Paradise. Either way…"

"You slept."

"Mostly."

"What do you mean, mostly?"

"Well, I'm in the woods in the dark at three in the morning. Every time I heard a noise, I jumped up and peeked out. Then I curled up and pretended to sleep again. I mean, really, would you sleep in an unlocked car in the middle of the woods alone?"

"Probably not, although I wouldn't put myself in an unlocked car in the middle of the woods all alone, you know why?" Rina shook her head. "Because, my dear, I would lock the doors."

Weston zigzagged across a few side streets, then turned onto a busy four-lane road.

"Where are we going?" Rina inquired. She wrapped her fingers together, then separated each, stretched, and did the same thing with the opposite hand on top.

"Someplace that will be safe for you," Weston said, staring straight ahead.

"Safe?"

"Yes, safe," he repeated.

"I need safety?"

"For now, you do."

Rina positioned her body to watch his every movement. Weston hadn't changed much since they dated. He still kept his sandy brown hair short, almost military length. He always had that great smile when he allowed himself to smile. Now he sat deep in thought, his puppy dog brown eyes darting at every turn.

Rina rested her gaze on his lips. She blushed at the thought of Weston connecting those luscious lips to hers, as the place under her skirt tingled. It had been a while since someone had given her a jolt down there. She looked back at Weston as he concentrated on driving, his strong, stubborn chin pointing the way. The last time she had seen him, she had watched that stubborn chin turn and walk away because she had refused to move to Alabama. "Seriously, Weston," she commented, "even the has-been-bands skip Alabama."

She looked down at her feet and began to laugh. There couldn't be two people more opposite. Her toe rings sparkled as she slid her feet out of worn Birkenstock sandals, and moved her tan legs into a crossed position. The purple gauze skirt rested just above her knees. Her dancing bear tie-dyed shirt had a few seam holes worn into it. The purple anklet moved to reveal a light tan line.

"I really should have left a note," she started giggling to break into the silence. "Doc is going to be pissed at me."

"Tangy, you really need to worry about yourself and not Doc right now."

"Neither one of us did anything wrong, except giving an asshole a ride," she answered. "And come on, we all could be guilty of that at some point in our lives." The scenery changed again. From oak canopied streets to significant roads, now into different buildings, one less descriptive as the next.

In the parking lot they pulled into, a black BMW sedan sat on the back of a flatbed truck. Rina couldn't see the license plate, but the voice in her head whispered: that's Docs. The car had no significant dents, scratches, or signs that would scream Doc's car. Yet Rina, who had just spent almost a week in and out of it, knew.

Weston turned into the entrance of an underground parking garage. If he hadn't turned, Rina would have missed the parking area altogether, as it was obscured by huge bushes with a matching green colored entryway.

"Things may get a little strange here," Weston instructed. "Just grab your backpack. You can get the case later." Rina took the bag by her feet. "How much stranger is this going to get?" She thought as she quickened her pace to match Weston's soldier step.

The empty gray hallway soon opened into a noisy office area. People rushed amid the maze of cubicles, but Weston cut straight down the middle. He nodded to several people and spoke to no one. Rina tried to keep track of the turns, but it felt like Weston was deliberately moving too quick for her to memorize the layout and hatch an escape plan.

When they broke through a glass door, things quieted down. An older, well-dressed woman sat up behind a tall desk. She greeted Wes as Mr. Traynor while appearing like she had been awaiting his arrival all day. She smiled as she handed over a stack of papers. Weston rifled through each while Rina and the woman smiled at each other. Weston looked up in time to catch their ill at ease glances.

"Oh, uh, sorry," He apologized to no one in particular. "Mary, Rina. Rina, Mary." The two women nodded and continued to smile at each other. "Rina is going to hang out in my office for a while. Please get her whatever she needs."

Mary nodded again. "Are you hungry? Can I get you something to drink? A soda, perhaps?"

"No, thank you," Rina replied as she followed Weston into his office. The spacious room opened up on one side into a floor to ceiling view of the spectacular Potomac River. A glass coffee table surrounded by two comfy neutral-toned couches filled half the room, giving the illusion of a quiet, upscale living room. A sizeable old-fashioned oak desk dominated the rest of the room. Between the two spaces, bookcases stood filled with awards and pictures and hardcover books.

Rina strolled around the office as Weston concentrated on his computer screen. She read the many plaques for outstanding service. At least half acknowledged some sort of military action in Iraq. Rina held on to herself to keep from reaching over to move anything for a better view. She stared at one of the photos labeled 1st Deployment. Weston stood with six other guys in full military gear. The date at the bottom read one week after their third and final break up.

She reread the date twice then put her hand to her stomach. He wanted a commitment because he was set to leave the country. He never told her that he wouldn't be staying with her in Alabama. She could have stayed in Connecticut with her family and went to concerts after all. Rina blew out a loud sigh. What did it matter now? Back then, she wanted things to stay just as they were for as long as possible. She didn't know if she could have handled being on her own, worrying about him all the time. She wanted to have fun, go to college, and see the world. Well, doing two out of three isn't bad. Rina's lips curved into a toothless smile.

The other plaques were for promotions and accommodations at his present position. The additional photographs contained mostly recreational activities. One in the front had been taken on a beach on some island with his family. Next to that was the standard ski resort photo: a group putting their arms around one another on a mountain in the winter. From every photo, faces looked out at Rina, and they were happy.

She glanced back, and when she noticed Weston engrossed in something on his desk, she reached over and moved the frame over about an inch. The date read Colorado two years ago. Interesting. She tried to remember when she had gotten the drunken phone call at four in the morning. Her mind wouldn't let her pinpoint a date, so she snuck a quick glance back at Weston, and then she went back to snooping. Another photo revealed Weston with some woman at a cocktail party. She was cute in a tall blonde model sort of way. Very well put together, one would say. Rina glanced at her own sandals and laughed.

In the back, hidden by another last-place trophy, sat a photo of Weston and his family on vacation. Rina sighed. She knew the photograph well because she had that same photo on a bookshelf at home. That was senior year, and his parents had rented a place at Misquamicut Beach in Rhode Island right on the water. They had invited her for the day. If it was the exact same photo, she thought it was, Weston and she stood arm in arm at the end, a view the trophy strategically blocked.

Rina held her elbows behind her back to keep from moving the frame for a closer look.

How could she still be on his bookshelf after all these years?

She sauntered over to the chair opposite his desk and plopped down. Her indigestion started to act up again. Weston looked up from his computer, and their eyes locked. The one who blinked first would lose. Her heart sped up.

"What?" he asked, not moving.

"Nothing," Rina wiggled in the chair to get comfortable. "Okay, something. I guess I'm confused. I mean, I was on my way to a stadium to see a concert. Then we had to make that stop because of the Asshole, and now I'm sitting here in your office, which is very nice, by the way," Weston nodded, "so I am wondering..."

Rina took in a deep breath as Weston asked, "wondering?"

"Yeah, wondering." She shook off his stare. "I mean, this is so freakin' weird." Rina got up and started to pace. The back of her neck got heated because she knew Weston's eyes were following her. "All I did was travel to some shows with my friend Doc who I have known forever..."

"You've known me forever. Doc is recent, but go on..."

"And now I'm here...with you...again..." Rina threw up her arms, "I'm not sure what is happening or where this rant is going. I'll probably lose my job…"

"You won't lose your job."

"Or my mind…"

"That I can't help you with," Weston laughed. "You lost that years ago."

"It's not funny, Wes. I have no way of getting home."

"You have a plane ticket in your backpack."

"And now I have no place to stay in DC." Rina sat down back down in the chair and breathed in heavy. Weston watched, his lips twisted in an amused smile.

"Rina, all those things are the least of your problems," Weston informed her. He shook his head. Same old Rina still focused on her world instead of the big picture.

Rina swallowed hard. "What do you mean?"

"Okay, let's start with the fact you are sitting in my office, and I work for a government agency that investigates drug trafficking," Weston stated.

"Yeah. But…"

"You were involved by the association in a major east coast meth bust."

"But, I thought that you saved from that…"

"Sort of."

"What do you mean sort of?"

"I'm getting there. So listen, I'm thinking that since you can't talk with this Dr. Jacko person, your tour people are probably going to peg you for a narc. I don't think that is a good thing, at least in my experience."

"You mean I can't go to any more shows?"

"Is that really what you're worried about?" Weston sat back and folded his arms over his chest. Although the situation was anything but funny, he laughed, "Same old Tangy."

"Stop calling me that, please."

Weston shrugged. Rina sat up, leaned forward, and rested her elbows on the edge of his desk. She took in a deep breath before starting. "I guess I really don't understand," she stated in a very calm voice. "I told you that Doc is a good guy and that other idiot," she shrugged. "He is the Asshole."

"And based on your word, I am supposed to let Doc go? Maybe put you guys up at the Grand Hyatt for your inconveniences? Or better yet, at the Watergate? I don't know. Do you need a spending allowance too? Backstage passes, and first-class plane tickets home?"

"Backstage passes? Really?" Rina's eyes watered.

"No," Weston replied, a bit more forceful than intended. "Yet, I might have a way for you to go and save face." Rina looked up in anticipation. She watched Weston's face relax a little and wasn't sure if that zing feeling meant she wanted to smother him in kisses or just smother him period.

"Save face with Doc or going to shows or both? Because right now, I'm a little," she sucked in a huge breath, "on edge."

"Look, Rina, I have never been to a show before, so what if you and I go together?"

"We could do that anyway."

"No. You'll go to the show, meet up with your friends, and act surprised when they tell you about Doc. You say you didn't know because you took off with your old boyfriend, who you still have the hots for."

Rina almost missed the last part. "How will they know about Doc?"

"Trust me. Word gets out when there is a glitch in the supply chain, and today, we created a major glitch." She considered how she would react to the news if she heard Doc got busted. Even now, the notion felt unreal.

"Come on, Tangy, I know you can act."

"Then what, you arrest all my friends?"

"Just the ones who are guilty." Weston leaned forward and took on a mirrored pose. His lips turned up into a savored smile. Rina winced. She had seen that look before, and it usually met trouble for her.

"You are not going to arrest my friends?" Weston shook his head side to side. "And you are not going to turn me into a narc?"

Weston reached across the desk, took Rina's hands, and gave them a gentle squeeze. His touch sent noticeable zings all over her body, and she blushed.

"Okay," she stated, then shook her head, because this was exactly how she lost her virginity.

"Okay!" He answered with a little too much enthusiasm for Rina. She looked back into his eyes. The zing changed to a flip-flop.

"Okay. If going to the show with you means helping Doc get out of this jam. Then yes, I will go to the concert with you."

"That was too easy," Weston leaned in close. The staring contest continued.

"So, can I go now?" Rina turned toward the door.

"Where?" Weston cocked his head to one side and waited. "Where could you possibly need to go?"

"I guess to a hotel. We were staying downtown, at a Marriott, I think, or maybe the Renaissance. That doesn't matter, though. It was pretty expensive, I remember, but that's not a big deal. I can just charge it and figure it all out later. Maybe find a couple of people to crash with me, you know…" Rina stopped to catch her breath. "So can I leave? I really need to check-in before they give our room away."

"Why not just hang out here? I got an hour or so of work left. You can watch TV, do whatever and then we can grab dinner and go."

"Yeah, except that I'm worried that if I don't go and grab the place now, the hotel will be sold out. You may not know this, but when the band comes to town that typically happens, you know, hotels selling out of rooms. Hum… Probably already are. Anyway, I think I should at least try," Rina stopped mid-sentence. In all her years of seeing the band, she had only slept in a parking lot once. She was in a Chevy Chevette with three other people, in Nowhere-Ville, Maryland, and she didn't want to be hotel-less ever again.

Weston watched as Rina placed each of her steps in front of the other, letting her foot linger in the air, then settling it into the carpet. He didn't move or interrupt her bouncing thoughts. Rina babbled non-stop. Babbling was a standard communication method for Rina, yet Weston knew the difference between standard and nerves. Her tone changed. Her arms flew up in the air, then floated back to her sides. The running commentary became more of a one-person dialog with random ideas discharging in every direction.

"Yeesh. I can not sleep in a car," Rina did a 360 on her right foot before continuing in the same direction. "I actually did that once, and it sucked besides, I don't have a car because like Doc drove and his car is wherever." She did a quick headshake. "So I should check the Marriott. I didn't make the reservation, though. I wonder if they would give me the room. You know, the front desk person might believe me that the room is mine, it just isn't in my name. The dude who booked it got arrested for drug trafficking, so instead of going to the waitlist, they should rent it to me as I'm supposed to be staying there either way. Of course, that won't work." She smacked her right hand against her forehead. "Then I'll have to find another place to stay… Unless you vouched for me, that could work. An FBI agent, or whatever you are now, should be a trustworthy source," Rina looked back into Weston's eyes, "…or maybe not." She went over by the couch to look out the window again.

"You know, Tangy, you could always stay with me."

"I don't think that's a good idea," Rina responded quickly. "And stop calling me that."

"Why, don't think you can keep your hands off me?"

"Yeah, right." Another zing passed through her body.

"Okay, let me be totally honest here," Weston leaned forward on his elbows again. "My ex Amber is moving her crap out as we speak."

"Uh-huh…" Amber must be the tall, put together blonde model in the photo. Of course, her name would be Amber. What else would it be? Rina sighed.

"Yeah, don't even ask. It is a very long story and a total waste of three years," Weston confessed. Rina didn't say anything, yet her heart tugged. Even now, she didn't like the idea of Wes being with someone else, especially when she was really, like in no prospects anywhere, single. "Maybe I'll tell you later."

She shook her head and laughed at the thought.

"Okay, maybe I won't," Weston smirked back. "But you would have your own space."

"My own space?"

"Yeah, I have a two-bedroom townhouse, and I don't use the bedroom on the top floor…"

"In the attic?"

"I guess if your image of an attic has a Jacuzzi and skylights."

"Jacuzzi and skylights?"

Weston released a deep sigh. "It was supposed to be the master bedroom. When I moved in, I got tired of lugging stuff upstairs, so I moved the main bedroom to the second floor. Now the top floor is the guest bedroom," Weston sucked in a huge breath and blew it out. "God, I forgot how exhausting you could be," he added.

"So you got lazy and made it a guest bedroom. What's up there, a cot?"

"No, Amber insisted on furnishing the top floor, so it has a bed, a bathroom, a closet. It's a standard room." Rina rolled her eyes. "You could even lock me out if you want."

The temperature of the room seemed to rise twenty degrees, as little balls of sweat ran between Rina's breasts. She spun around in the opposite direction in hopes of creating some sort of breeze. She bit her bottom lip. The longer she waited, the narrower her choices became.

"Tell you what. Let me call a few folks to see if I could hook up with anyone of my friends." Rina turned during the last part and watched Weston shake his head no. "I do have friends, you know." Weston didn't reply. "Can I at least get in touch with some people to let them know I am staying with a friend?"

"Are these people your family?" Weston asked. Rina shook her head no. "Yeah, no, you can't."

"But why?" Rina wailed, just as Mary appeared in the doorway, to see the young one throwing a hissing fit. At the same time, the boss, as usual, attempted to control the situation. Perhaps this one would give her trouble after all.

Mary hadn't liked Amber. She treated her like the help. Still, this one was more polite, even though she was a bit on the weird side.

"Excuse me, sir," Mary interrupted. "Did you need anything else? It's almost four, and I need to..." she nodded toward the exit.

"Nope, we are good, Mary. Thanks."

"It was nice meeting you," Rina replied.

"You too," answered Mary. "See you tomorrow." She disappeared into the outer office.

"No offense, but I hope that 'see you tomorrow' was for you, because I ain't coming back here."

"Tangy..."

"No, really. I think I'll just take my stuff on the metro to Washington National, and I'll fly home."

"That's not a good idea," Weston stood and shuffled papers on his desk.

"And why isn't it a good idea?" Rina went back to fighting tears and biting her bottom lip.

"Come on, Tangy..."

"Stop calling me that!"

"Seriously. You know why it's not a good idea. If we needed you back here to answer questions, we would have to issue a warrant. Please trust me. Remember how you used to trust me." Rina stopped mid-stride.

"What choice did I have?"

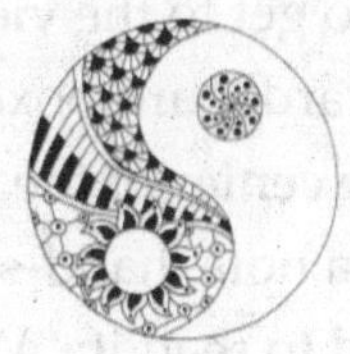

Rina stood in the open space of Weston's townhouse and stared out the window, mesmerized by the view. His office building stood in the far distance, separated by a river, a highway, and a cemetery. The view from his house was almost the complete reverse of the view from his office. Rina wondered if he even noticed.

She had been surprised to drive through the dilapidated urban area to get here. Homeless people pushed the shopping carts that held their life past burned-out brick buildings and strange graffiti. Weston's building had an underground parking garage, which secured the tenants and their vehicles from the surrounding mob.

The building itself was nothing special. Old and brick, at one time it could have been a factory or at least the office portion of a factory. Rina liked that Weston's section of town was being redeveloped. She noted there are already a couple of restaurants, a dry cleaner, and a small grocer on his block. It showed promise.

Rina leaned against the glass doors that opened to a small balcony. The balcony hung over a busy highway. To get to the view, she walked around a stack of cardboard boxes, each had a perfect label, in the center of the room. In the middle, there was a note, hand-scribbled. Of course, she glanced to read it: "Weston, the movers, will be by tomorrow for the rest. Have a good…"

Rina walked straight to the windows wondering how the note should end. Have a good life? Day? A cup of coffee?

"Those should be gone," Weston scowled at the mess. Rina was about to point at the note then stopped. He'll figure it out. "So, I have three floors here," Weston started up the stairs. "You can see the first. The second should still have all my stuff, and you can take the third. There is a separate staircase from the third floor to the first…"

Rina looked back, "Huh?"

"Just follow me," Weston said, adding, "please" as an afterthought. Rina turned to follow him up a narrow spiral staircase. The stairs bent around the back of the fireplace and led up to a landing. Weston carried both her backpack and the roadie case.

"Hey, I need those," Rina instructed. "At least I need the case for the show." She bit her lower lip as Weston gave her the death stare.

"That is if I decide to go…" This was one of the looks she had helped him perfect in high school. He would just give a blank stare as if Rina could just read his mind and adhere to his wishes. His wishes back then usually meant he was getting hot for her. His look today revealed more frustration than sex appeal.

Seeing the stare, Rina explained, "Fine. I have my tape deck in there. To, you know, tape the show. See Doc, and I are tapers. We go in, sit in a special section, and record the show." Weston's eyes widened. "It is totally legit. We bootleg," she watched Weston flinch, "Okay, bad choice of words, but we have the bands' permission. It's a whole section, not just me and Doc…"

Weston put the roadie case by the stairs and rubbed the space between his eyes. "It's really not illegal," Rina pleaded. She reached into the front pocket of her backpack and held out her two show tickets for Weston to see. "See right on the ticket, it says 'taper.'"

"So it does," nodded Weston. Rina brushed up against his arm as she put the tickets back in the front pocket. Weston flinched with her touch. Not enough for her to notice, yet enough for him to get a jolt. "So, this is the second floor," he focused on his surroundings. "Oh shit."

"You are a bit messy there." The room was covered in clothes. There were clothes on the bed—clothes on the floors. And, of course, clothes folding out of drawers, closets, and even baskets. The room looked like someone had ransacked it.

"Yeah, not me." Weston moved to the staircase on the other side. "Okay, so this is going to be your space. As I said, you can lock the door, or whatever." Rina trudged up another staircase and then gasped as she hit the top landing. A grand space opened before her. An enormous bed was the centerpiece, decorated in a white bedspread with white throw pillows scattered at the headboard. A large window peaked out over the river and the highway but was fashioned, so one saw only the distant river. A large skylight illuminated the entire room with the last of the day's golden sunlight.

The opposite wall was lined with white enameled panel doors. Weston opened the closest entrance to show a stack of fluffy, white towels. Next, he opened the door into the enormous white bathroom with a tub butted up against the far wall, beneath a large frosted glass window.

In the corner stood another shower, with jets on all sides. "I think I'm falling in love," she reached out for the shower spout. "We had one of these in Orlando last spring." She ran her hand over the glass door. "I could have actually stayed in Florida just to use a shower like this every day."

Weston coughed, "Okay, here we have the closet. Bathroom. Closet. Back stairway."

"Wow, I meant what I said," Rina replied, still entranced with the shower. In almost a whisper, she continued, "Maybe it wasn't Orlando, but I am sure it was Florida. Wait, I know, we had this shower in the hotel down in Miami last year. Yeah, Miami. The shower became my best friend. I didn't want to leave the hotel, not even for the shows. Really, I could have married that shower."

"The room came this way," he added by explanation. Weston moved next to Rina, and together they turned to look into the mirror at the same time. *Zing.*

"All righty then," Weston broke the spell. "I'll be ready to go in a few."

"Go where?"

"The concert."

"Concert?"

"I thought you wanted to go to the show..."

"Oh yeah," Rina said as she looked back around the room. "Yeah, I guess I can shower later. Yeah. Let's just go to the show." She watched Weston disappear down the stairs and moved her backpack to the chest at the foot of the bed. Rina then sat cross-legged on the bed and stared at the wall, where a photograph of a non-descript lighthouse took up most of the view. She leaned forward and pulled a bag of hippie trail mix out from the front part of her backpack. Rina sorted the M & M's out from amongst the almond pieces, oats, sunflower seeds, and flax. Her friend Luna made and bagged the stuff to sell on tour. Luna had a secret ingredient that made you want more and more, but she guaranteed to Rina that it wasn't illegal.

"I get drug tested for my job at the casino, you know."

"You are safe, chickee-poo. So safe," Luna had said with a wink. Luna and Rina had a lot in common. She worked in the city doing something that apparently made her gobs of money — the trail mix thing she did for fun. "Lets me meet lots of people," Luna explained one time. Rina just nodded, though, in the back of her mind, she thought there had to be a better way to meet people unless, of course, you wanted to find yourself in some kind of trail mix-lovers club.

Rina stretched out on the bed and watched the clouds float by. A big puff of white trailed across the tranquil blue sky. The blob just puffed along, leaving a trail of little puffs that soon faded into the blue.

Rina's thought turned toward Doc. Where was he? Was he safe? She popped another M&M

into her mouth and tried to remember what Wes had said. Doc was in big trouble. What the heck did that mean? The white baby cloud puffs faded, and soon the mother cloud went beyond her view.

Rina closed her eyes and started to picture her journey here. In Queens, they stopped on the street that resembled a photo from Beirut instead of a borough of New York. Busted windows in burnt outbuildings. People with vacant eyes stopped and stared at Doc's car. Rina would reach over and check the door lock with each approach.

Doc had stayed in the car with her and kept the engine running the entire time. He had kept whispering, "Come on already," after the first few minutes. When the Asshole finally got back into the car, they drove away really fast. Rina remembered a terrible boom just before they hit the bridge back to Manhattan. The rumble shook the car a little too. She was never so happy in her life to be heading onto the island.

After checking into the Fairmount, Doc had wanted to head out to dinner. Rina politely declined and ordered a room service salad. After, she locked herself in the smaller of the two bedrooms the suite featured. She managed to sleep a little, even after the party started. Laughter, loud voices, and music slipped under her door, yet the tiny voice in her head told her to stay put. People had jiggled the door handle several times throughout the night. Each vibration or loud knock jolted her awake again. Louder and louder, the little voice inside her head screamed, "Do not open that door." Rina always listened to that voice. Ever since she learned the hard way, Rina was diligent in following her inner voice's directive.

Her wariness started at check-in. They usually stayed at a Marriott with the occasional Hilton thrown in. Last summer, they drove an hour each way to stay at a Marriot in Nowhere-Ville, Maine, instead of the Holiday Inn next to the venue. It turned out to be the same Holiday Inn where the band stayed. She and Doc joked that they had a nicer place than the band. Then again, Rina guessed it didn't matter. In any case, that Marriott was totally overboard, even for Doc.

Rina rolled onto her stomach and moved, so her head hung off the side of the bed. This allowed her entire body to lie flat. A thick purple colored rug surrounded the bed and butted up to a spotless hardwood floor. Not even a dust bunny dared to enter this space.

She shut her eyes and let her mind wander. Even though she had seen the photo in his office, Rina tried to imagine what Amber looked like. Blonde? Brunette? Pretty? Of course, she was beautiful. She was with Weston. A soft smile formed on her lips as thoughts of Weston entered her subconscious. They were a cute couple back in the day.

Rina rolled over eyes wide open. She shook her head to banish the thought. That part of her life ended long ago. She refocused on her current state. What a waste of a day this turned out to be! Instead of playing Frisbee or hacky sack in the sunshine, she was stuck inside an apartment. She should be exploring the parking lot, dancing to a different song every few feet, or napping on a blanket by the car while she soaked up a tan. Doc would be kicking back in the rusty old lawn chair he hauled around from show to show. They had been joking about buying a new one, but Doc always said, "Not until this one falls apart beneath me."

Doc would be mellowed with a glass of wine or maybe sharing a joint with Cowboy — if Cowboy even bothered to show up.

"Holy crap," Rina sat upright. Cowboy. That was her ticket. She would find Cowboy during the show, tell him what happened, and he would know exactly what to do. The last few shows, Cowboy had been hanging around with Doc and her in the pit, and maybe tonight she would get lucky, and he would show up again. The thought of being happy to see Cowboy made her laugh since it was normal for them to fight like siblings with Doc refereeing.

This could work. Now that Rina had a plan, she laid back down, closed her eyes, and drifted off to the clouds.

Weston went back down to the second floor. He started to pick his clothes up and return everything to its rightful drawer or hanger. At the start, he took the time to fold each piece and place it in the correct spot. Still, after five minutes, he gave up and started shoving shirts, sweats, and underwear back into random dresser drawers.

Wes stared at the picture on top of his dresser. It was of Amber and him holding each other at an office party last year. But now the glass on the frame was shattered. The fact that she took the time to smash the glass then return the frame to its place on the dresser confirmed that Weston had made the right decision in asking her to leave. Discovering his old flame Tangerina was traveling with an east coast drug king, also confirmed it.

Tangy and Amber would not have fit comfortably in his life. Both women were high maintenance in their own unique way. Tangy was too head strung for her own good, yet she could be silly. Amber was never foolish. Everything had to be just so, or all hell would break loose. When Weston asked why he would get what he had named the Bitch Stare. Hands-on her slim hips, head slightly bent forward, lips turned down in a scowl, and eyes were blazing into his. There was no match for Amber's Bitch Stare.

Weston smiled as he tried to imagine both women in the same space at the same time. Even his imagination couldn't get there. He opened the top drawer and pulled out an old wooden picture frame. Smiling back at him were two kids standing on a beach. One in jean cut-offs and the other in a purple bikini. Her long sun-streaked hair was tied back in a high ponytail. Goofy smiles were frozen on both faces. Weston touched the photo and then put it back in its place.

He went down to the kitchen, filled a glass with water, and then turned on his laptop. He sat with his back to the view, logged on, and waited. After a couple of sips of water, the screen came alive. First, the official agency logo came up, then after a few clicks, his email system. Weston selected the subject line "Operation Slimebag," and waited. He read the report and sighed.

The report stated that neither party was talking at this point. His team knew that getting Jacko to talk was vital. He had one rogue agent plus the credibility of his entire squad riding on this bust. He typed an email, "Tangerina is with me. I pulled her from the scene. I will try to find out what she knows and get back to you tonight. Thank you again for the option." Weston hit send, reread the report, and closed up the laptop. He finished the water then turned toward the view out the sliding doors. The pieces were starting to fall together, and although he was seasoned at his job, he didn't like the direction that leads were pointing in.

Could there be two traitors on his team, and if so, how to flush out the second? Bringing in Jacko might help if he spoke. Did he really want to use Tangy for the next step? He sighed and looked up at the ceiling. Could he do what he needed to to get what he wanted?

Weston put the glass in the dishwasher then headed upstairs.

It was almost showtime.

Weston watched Rina sleep from the top of the stairs. Her body formed a perfect C, and, just as he remembered, she smiled as she slumbered. A warm sensation moved up his body. If he had to confess under oath, he would have no trouble admitting that he had missed her all these years. He said a quick prayer, asking for help in keeping her safe.

Reluctantly he moved toward the bed and sat on the edge. Weston reached out to rub Rina's back. She was warm. He leaned over and took a deep inhale of flowers, musk, and maybe a touch of patchouli. His eyes got blurry. He shook away the stars and focused back on Rina.

"Come on, Tangy – time to get up," he said. Rina stretched her arms over her head while she turned on her back. The smile remained.

"Why?" she whined.

"Show tickets, you know…"

"Oh yeah," Rina sat up, shook her head, and looked around the room. "Nice hotel."

"Tangy, this is not a hotel, it is my place, remember?"

"Damn, I thought that all was just another nightmare." Rina slid off the opposite side of the bed then disappeared into the bathroom. "So when are we going to show?" she asked behind the closed door.

"Whenever you are ready," Weston replied. He heard the toilet flush, and the water turn on and off.

Rina floated back into the room, grabbed her bright green flip-flops, and said, "Let's go," with much more enthusiasm than she had. Waking up next to Weston had thrown her off balance. Although Doc was on her mind, Weston had crept back into her dreams.

The advantage of having an FBI agent drive you to a concert is that he passes traffic, runs through red lights and roadblocks, and cuts down the time it takes to get to your destination. The disadvantage is that you have to ride in an official government vehicle. The ride from Weston's townhouse to RFK took less than twelve minutes. Rina would have been sitting in the standstill traffic jam of concertgoers for at least another hour when Weston pulled into the gate backstage.

Rina focused on the fact that she got a ride to the show from an FBI agent. And as fate would have it, this wasn't just any old investigator. This was the agent investigating one of her friends. And the investigator happened to be her ex-love, not just any love, but THE love. The only thing worse than that would be arriving at a concert with a DEA agent and dogs.

Weston pulled around to the back of the stadium, flashed his ID, and moved around some orange cones to park near a line of similar-looking cars. Actually, every vehicle in the row was identical to the next.

"What do you people do," Rina asked, "buy in bulk?"

Weston smiled and watched her stare at his license plate. Her lips moved slowly, then she shut her eyes to make the same movements.

"What are you doing?"

"I am memorizing the license plate. In case I get lost, or we get separated." She kept her focus on the letters. "I have a strange feeling I don't want to be stuck here."

"You won't be," Weston replied. "I'll come to find you."

"Oh, so you won't be hanging with me?" Rina half flirted. She couldn't decipher between disappointment at the fact that Weston decided to ditch her or relief that he wasn't going to be around, and she could try to find Cowboy. She felt a similar tug-of-emotions when they split up too.

Weston took Rina's hand and led her over to a small desk. He proceeded to chat up the woman on the other side while he rubbed his thumb over the top of Rina's wrist. The woman smiled seductively back at Weston as she handed him an envelope. He took out two fluorescent green backstage passes. Once she inspected the passes, Rina was quick to note that these were not the band's backstage passes, which always had some sort of unique and colorful designs, but instead some other, less influential badges.

"I get a backstage pass? Cool!" Rina couldn't wait to show it off to Cowboy. He and Doc often got backstage and, at times, would lend the pass to her so she could try to get a glimpse of her favorite band members. Sometimes, they let her keep the pass, and she pasted them into a scrapbook annotated with memories from the show.

"I can go visit the band with this?" Weston placed the pass in her hand.

"No," came in stereo. The desk woman changed from hot for Weston to concern that she would have to keep an eye on Rina.

"This will get you around the stage and back to here," Weston explained. "But don't worry… I will find you at the stadium if I need to."

Rina gave Weston her toothless-smile, her way of saying kiss-off.

Weston rested his arm around Rina's shoulder as he guided her toward a long tunnel hallway. Rina carried the pass in her hand until some guy with a buzz cut instructed otherwise.

"You need to wear that, miss."

With dramatic flair, Rina dropped the roadie case, pulled the backing off, and slapped the pass on to her skirt.

"We prefer you to wear it on your shirt," the buzz cut responded. "Upper left corner."

Weston put his hand over Rina's mouth before she could reply. "Yeah – but now you get to check out her legs when she comes by," he said

The buzz cut laughed out loud while Rina turned crimson. "Cute," she responded. "Really cute."

When the buzz cut started to comment, Weston held up one hand, and buzz cut was silenced.

"Wish I could do that to him," Rina muttered.

Weston directed Rina toward the tunnel leading through several poorly lit corridors. Faint smells of garbage and urine filled the air. The long dank hallway popped out about halfway across the coliseum, conveniently right by Rina's seats. She let out a sigh of relief when Cowboy's long, lean body was lounging next to a couple of empty seats. Cowboy just cracked her up. With his short, brown hair, golf shirts, and pressed jeans, he created this illusion of respectability. Yet, there was nothing preppy or responsible about him. With not a crease in his clothing or a hair out of place, he stood out in a crowd of long hair and tie-dyes.

"Okay, well, I'm going to my seats," Rina said, trying to disengage Weston's hand.

"Not a word about Jacko, Tangy," Weston said with his cop face on. If you have ever been pulled over for speeding, you know the look: hard jaw, no humor in the eyes, just plain intimidating. Rina rolled her eyes up to the ceiling. "I'm serious, Rina. I don't want to have to arrest you after saving your ass."

Rina opened then closed her mouth several times before replying, "I'll meet you here after the show." She turned to go, but Weston pulled her back. Their bodies slammed together, and he crushed his mouth over hers. As much as Rina wanted to push away, her body gave in, softening with his touch. Explosions of purples, blues, and greens went off in her mind as she tasted sweets from her past. Her brain tried to push her body away, yet her arms failed to follow instructions.

When Weston broke away, she staggered a bit and looked up into his eyes. "Have fun," he said with a smile and disappeared into the tunnel. Rina stood still for a moment and breathed heavy. She didn't dare move until her breath and legs were steady.

As Weston blended into the darkness, she muttered "Bastard," then headed towards Cowboy.

Weston was grateful for the darkness. He hadn't intended to kiss Rina again, but in some ways, he couldn't help himself. From back in the day as young tenth graders, she had always been the one for him, and he never could get enough of those lips. Now, here she was years later, and the opportunity, although slim, existed to recreate what Weston considered to be a perfect romance. Even while dating others, Amber included, he kept mementos of Rina around. There was the friendship bracelet she sent him during the off-years sitting in a ceramic bowl here, and a framed snapshot of her over there. Their relationship hadn't been perfect, yet he based all others on what he and Rina had. Unfortunately for Weston, no other relationship measured up.

After a couple of deep breaths, his lips stopped shaking. He made his way to the makeshift office his team had put together and reassumed his professional, non-demonstrative, composure.

"Ok, what do we got?" he asked the room cramped with people. Last week it was custodian's closet, now it was home base, complete with a six-foot folding table and a dozen folding chairs. A large screen hung from the far end of the room, displaying blown-up photos of Doc, Jacko, and two other men being led away from the apartment in handcuffs.

When Beman stood up and began speaking, the other agents grabbed chairs and quieted down.

"You know the first person, the driver, Bruce Norton from Massachusetts. The second is our target Jacko Manilla, last address an apartment in Kittery, Maine. This is who we believed to have the distribution list or at least know of its whereabouts. Our buddy Tony is next," several people reached over to slap their colleague on the back, "And then we have Lyle Tremont. No current address and very little information." Beman turns towards Weston, "We think that Tremont may be the agency connection. At least that is what we are working on now."

"What about Jacko?" Weston asked, staring at the photo.

"It looks like he is just a small-time dealer at this point. It seems our intelligence may be bad." Weston shook his head.

"I find that difficult to believe," Weston responded.

"Sorry, boss, but all the new info says…"

"Did you get the case out of the Bemer?" Weston interrupted.

"What case?" Beman asked.

"There wasn't a government-issued briefcase in the trunk?"

"Not that we found. There was just a bunch of backpacks and recording equipment, why? Did you see anything else?"

Weston hesitated before replying, "I must not have. There was a lot of crap back there." The group laughed in agreement. "Okay, who is on our radar tonight?"

"We know who is on your radar," Agent Wilson joked, and when no one laughed, he muttered, "Sorry, boss."

The next slide showed a photo of a tall, lanky kid. "This is Neil Moon, also known as the Cowboy. He was sitting in the seats near where Doc was to be tonight." Click. "This is Luna, we don't have another name. She sells trail mix and marijuana. We are not sure of her connection, yet she is tied in somehow. And last," Rina's photo came up on the screen.

"This is Tangerina Hanley," Weston started to say. "Also known as Rina. We are not sure of the connection here, yet we are looking into it." There were a couple snickers in the room. "And yes, for those of you not privy to office gossip, Ms. Hanley and I dated in high school. For the record, this investigation is the first time I have seen her in five years." Weston paused and waited. "I am keeping my personal life separate. If anyone in this room feels otherwise, I expect you to speak now or keep your peace." Silence filled the air. "Mary will continue to coordinate all information. Please put her on all correspondence."

"What is next, boss?"

"Let's see what Rina is up to and keep a close watch on this Cowboy character. We side with caution here, folks," Weston added as the sounds of chairs scraping the floor filled the air.

"Yo," Cowboy barked through half-closed eyes at the same time Rina plopped down in the chair next to him. Rina noted the microphone stand was already set up and wired to Cowboy's DC-5, the gold standard of bootleg tape decks.

"Yo, back at ya," Rina answered while she fidgeted her case open. She pulled from the foam her own DC-5, an earlier version of Cowboy's. Being a trust fund kid or Trustafarian, as they were commonly referred to on tour, Cowboy had the luxury of getting the latest and greatest electronics along with other perks like free flights, rental cars, and let's not forget the all-important Marriott stays, because of his gene pool. Rina, on the other hand, would have to work a double shift of dealing card in a smoky casino just to afford the next model down, never mind the travel perks.

She took off the battery case and proceeded to put in fresh batteries and a new connector wire.

"Cowboy, how stoned are you?" She staged whispered.

"The usual," Cowboy shrugged. He looked around and wondered out loud, "Where is the Doctor?"

"That is what I am trying to find out," Rina replied through gritted teeth. She looked over her shoulder toward the tunnel entrance, then scanned the crowd. With no sign of Weston, she continued, "That's what I am trying to find out," she leaned closer to Cowboy. "We were traveling with the Asshole…"

"There's your first mistake," he smiled and held up one finger.

"Then, my old boyfriend from high school…"

"Uh? Old boyfriend, huh? Intriguing," he started moving his head to a beat only he could hear.

"Who happens to work for the FBI," now that got Cowboy to lean in closer, "Dude, be discreet. They are all over the place here." Cowboy nodded and sat back.

"What was your FBI agent-ex doing hanging out with you and the Doctor?"

In a low voice, Rina repeated the entire adventure from Manhattan to the present. Cowboy didn't say anything yet when she looked back into his eyes, for the first time since she met him, the Cowboy appeared alert. He caught her gaze, took in a deep breath, and then closed his eyes. His breathing became rhythmic. Rina waited while Cowboy reached into his case and pulled out his pipe. Without fanfare, he lit the pipe and inhaled deep. With the same breathing patterns as before, he held the smoke for a ten count then exhaled slow. Then he turned back to Rina.

"We have got to get the Doctor," he stage whispered back.

"How? I don't know where they took him or the Asshole."

"You need to find out," Cowboy instructed, as the band walked across the stage with no fanfare. Notes of music floated through the building as each musician warmed up and tuned their instruments. Rina wondered why they never did this before the audience arrived.

"Hey, I just thought of a twofer. Like maybe you could have sex with your ex and con it out of him," Cowboy laughed. "I'm just kidding. You are probably not that good."

Rina reached over and smacked Cowboy on the side of his head. "Jackass…"

"Hey!" Cowboy went to grab tapes out of his backpack. "That's a good idea."

"I didn't say anything," Rina said in a low tone as the Cowboy stood to leave.

"You pay attention and do the flips. I will be right back."

Rina grabbed Cowboy's arm, "Where are you going?"

"I'm going to find those meth-head idiots that the Asshole hangs out with. Maybe I can persuade one of them to tell me what is going on." Cowboy fist-bumped Rina and left her to watch the show.

"Never thought I'd miss the Cowboy," she commented to no one. Then as the band started into its first bluesy number, Rina leaned over to press play on both tape decks. She looked back at the exit tunnel in time to catch Weston looking out at her. Though he blended into the shadows, Rina could feel the heat of his gaze. Her heart pumped faster and whispered to run into his arms, but the louder voice in her head urged caution.

Bodies swirled into different colors around her as dancers took to the floor and moved to the tribal beat. She looked back and caught Weston's eye. He stepped out of the shadows and smiled in Rina's general direction. For a moment, she glanced back at the image on her camcorder, and when she peeked again, he was gone. Just an illusion, she told herself, try to enjoy the music. Both arms hugged her hips while her perpetual smile disappeared from her lips.

Rina searched the area for a glimpse of Cowboy but found him nowhere in sight. Working in the casino helped her refine her peripheral vision. This also helped while walking to the car after late-night shifts, heightening her overall ability to sense danger. Even after years of traveling with Doc, Rina only relaxed while the music played. Her personality went from hyper to mellow with the first plucks of the guitar strings.

Tonight her stomach ached, and her head hurt. PMS didn't even bring on this type of pain. Rina sighed. She looked at the dancers, then back to the band. Usually, she would be drifting off to dance in a corner now. Still, here she was scanning the taper's section for familiar faces. Cowboy filled her thoughts. Where the heck was he? And when would he be back? Rina looked around to see the Mini Maglites shining around her. It must be time to flip the tape. She sighed again. This was supposed to be Doc's job. She was not allowed near the tape decks until it was time for pack up. Doc and Cowboy thought she'd get too into the music and space through the flip.

Rina reached in Cowboy's backpack to search for his Maglite. Cowboy and Doc held the flashlight in their mouth, which Rina wouldn't do. "Too phallic," she'd bark at the boys. She placed the light on the ground, waiting for the song to end. She pressed stop on both tape decks, flipped the tapes, then pressed play and record together. Another sigh escaped her lips. "At least they can say I got the flips right," she mumbled to the mic stand.

As Rina congratulated herself, something heavy pushed down in the middle of her back. It forced her back into her chair. She turned her head to see a pair of black converse sneakers disappear into khaki-gray pants. The pressure on her back moved up to her neck.

"Look at me," a gravel voice rattled through her head. "I said, look at me!" The sound got louder as a jolt of pain shot through her neck. Rina turned her head. A skinny guy with rage-filled eyes bore into hers. He wore a gray suit along with a rainbow rasta wig. Though she didn't notice him slide into the tapers' section, his hard fingers on her neck became a harsh lesson to be more observant.

Rina wanted to run. She didn't know this person. She would have remembered those meth-dead eyes. She tried to stay away from the meth heads as much as possible. They were just too messed up and too weird — even for Rina.

The bearded man raised his head to look around. As the light hit the side of his face, Rina noticed a quiet scar running down his left cheek. Thin and barely noticeable, she made a note just in case she ever saw this person without the wig. The eyes and the scar would stay with her.

Her breaths came quick. Her head spun in circles. *He's going to kill me right here.*

"Now listen," he started up again. "I don't know where your friends are hiding, but they were supposed to bring me something," his breath reeked like rotting metal. "And I want my stuff!" He tightened his grasp for emphasis on the word stuff. Rina squeaked.

"You tell that asshole and his idiot friend," He continued, "that I am not a person to screw with!" He moved his hand from Rina's neck to graze her cheek. She shivered. "Or," with a crooked, toothless smile, he added, "Pretty little girls disappear."

Rina's mouth fell open. The stranger, who she immediately nicknamed in her head Meth Head Biker Dude, stumbled out of the taper's section. Rina stood to look in all directions. *Where the heck was Cowboy? Or Weston? What the heck! Wasn't Wes supposed to be watching me?* She hoped to spy a familiar face amongst the crowd, and none were to be found. Rina gripped her waist in a feeble attempt to stop the shakes. To passersby, her movements couldn't have looked too far off from the meth heads who held themselves to keep together in between fixes.

Flashlights sparkled on the ground around her, yet Rina just tried to breathe normally. She jumped, as a tap on her shoulder sent convulsions through her body.

"Yo, Rina," a familiar voice told her. "End of the first set. You need to stop the decks and switch stuff out." Rina nodded and went through the motions. She popped the first set tape out and threw both copies into Cowboy's backpack. She then opened new tapes and placed each inside. With a deep sigh, she sat back.

"Where's the Doctor and Cowboy?" the guy behind her asked. Rina couldn't remember his name, yet she had seen him around before. Doc talked to almost everyone, so they all knew him. She, on occasion, stayed in the taper's section. However, since the Asshole joined the tour, Rina disappeared amongst the dancers instead of being in his company.

"Don't know," she answered.

"Isn't it weird for the two of them to leave you here?"

"Yeah, maybe they went backstage or something." With a shrug, she added, "I don't know."

"Just I've never seen them leave you before," the guy rambled. "Thought it was, you know weird, but then again, Doc and Cowboy are different…" She turned to scan the crowd while the guy behind her rambled on about Doc, Cowboy, and the night's first set. Like with sports, the analysis takes place prior, during, and after each show. Rina finally focused her attention on the tunnel, where a lone police officer stood in front of the shadows.

Rina watched reunions take place all around. Arms flew around people, along with warm hugs shared. Smiles shone brightly. She caught a glimpse of rainbow rasta wigs floating throughout the coliseum.

Her foot tapped, and her head spun. Cowboy still hadn't come back. "This just sucks," she muttered. No one seemed to notice as the folks behind her sat back and smoked a joint. Rina let out a loud sigh, sat down, and pouted.

Weston moved through the dim-lit corridors. The light shown from under one of the doors, and as he opened it, temporary blindness took over. "Damn," he muttered as he moved to take one of the empty seats at the table. The wall in front was stacked with monitors as dozens of cameras streamed different areas of the arena.

Weston squinted to focus on the bottom left screen. He watched as Rina chatted with the lanky person next to her—the Cowboy. Her eyes darted around as she spoke.

"She's telling him about Jacko," he said.

"How do you know, boss?"

"She keeps looking over her shoulder, probably for me…" The room erupted in howls. "That is not my ego talking. I warned her about mentioning the arrest before she left, but Rina has listening issues."

"You mentioned that at the bust."

Snickers filled the room. "She's telling him about Jacko, I know it." After a few more minutes, the Cowboy departed.

"Follow him," Weston instructed. A person close to the door got up and walked out. Weston didn't turn to see who it was, because he was watching Rina.

"What is our plan?"

"We wait," Weston said. "If Rina is involved, she is going to lead us right to the list and maybe the source..."

"And if she is not involved?" Mary asked. Weston hesitated before looking direct at Mary.

"Then, hopefully, the source will come to her, and we can get the information that way." Weston showed no emotion, yet his assistant felt the anxiety across the room. She watched him fold his arms, then switch, which was on the top, and refold. Weston had a reputation for being calm, even in the highest pressured situations. To Mary, he looked anything but.

She observed the other agents in the room. Not one took notice of her boss's fidgety movements. That was good. Maybe he'd lead them to the promised land after all. Weston's eyes darted back and forth between Rina sitting up her microphones and the images of Cowboy walking across various monitors.

The kid could move. Weston noted that both Cowboy and his agent drifted through the crowds pretty easily. His fashion sense helped, his solids standing out all too easy amongst the sea of spirals. Two of Weston's agents appeared on and off the screens. One was Beman, who blended in well with the crowd in full-on hippie get up. The other was a new hire from drug enforcement. Weston looked back at Rina and smiled. She sat back with her arms folded across her chest. Several times he watched her hold up her hands and shake her head no to the stoner who sat behind her. *I don't do that crap* echoed in his mind.

His crew had done a spectacular job in a short amount of time. He had to negotiate with everyone from the band to the promoter to the venue operators to accomplish this. The group requested no cameras on the bus. Their dressing rooms and buffet areas were both empty. His team agreed that during the time the band was in town, their busses would be considered a sovereign nation, at least for now.

Weston figured if the person they were looking for was actually involved with the band, they would be seen leaving the bus or loitering in the general vicinity. The stagnant camera on Rina was said to be there to catch her cohorts. That was what Weston put on the design form. In reality, he wanted to keep an eye on her to keep her safe.

The only place in the building they didn't put some kind of camera was the restrooms. The rest of the building was in full view. Twenty-five screens surrounded the wall in front of him. Half were positioned on a particular area while the rest looped through several places. He found his agents all wandering in circles. All except Beman, that is. "Now where did he go," Weston mumbled out loud.

"Hey boss, something's up with the kid."

Weston turned around in his chair. "What do you mean something's up?" He stared down Beman. "Why are you here?"

"Because I thought you should know I followed him through the hallway, and then he just disappeared."

"Disappeared," Weston started to shake his head, a nervous habit he used only when thoroughly agitated. "How the hell can he just disappear?"

"I caught up to him in the hallway, then a whole bunch of people crowded the hall..."

"And you lost him in the crowd?"

"Yes and no. I thought I did, then I saw him head into the bathroom on the third floor. I went in there, but it was empty."

"Empty?"

"Yeah." Weston stared wide-eyed at Conrad Beman. *This couldn't be happening again.* Beman had proven to be one of his best agents in the short amount of time they had been together, yet his story sounded weak. He counted to ten and waited for his partner to continue.

"I don't get how it could be empty either…"

Weston took in an extra-deep breath. "Okay, I want a couple of folks to comb that area." His finger jammed against the screen, "Try to find Mr. Cowboy. When you find him, bring him in."

"On what charges?" Mary asked.

"I'm sure he has marijuana or something on him. I don't care. He looks like a guy we are looking for. Make up something. Just bring him in and anyone who is with him."

"What about her?" Beman asked.

"Just keep an eye on her," Weston replied as he headed for the door. "Let me know who she's hanging out with." Weston headed off toward the elevators as Conrad Beman took over the command center.

"Okay, boys, you heard the boss. Let's find the Cowboy." The group moved toward the door. "Mary will watch the monitors while we have a look around." Conrad winked in Mary's direction.

The door closed behind him. "I need you guys to hit the third tier and see what you could find," Conrad instructed as he took off in the opposite direction.

Cowboy made his way up to the third-floor rafters. He turned several times to see the same long hairs behind him. Without warning, he swooped down into the crowd and made his way to the men's room.

Hippies bounced in and out, yet none were part of the Asshole's circle, so he made his way up to the next floor. The users of the hard stuff tended to all hang out together in the quietest spot in the concert hall. Oddly enough, that was also where the young mothers tended to congregate with their little ones. Toddlers would stumble around the bodies folded against the walls. Between smoker's coughs, the only sound vibrating off the walls were the giggles and overtired wails of children.

Cowboy had always wondered if the young mothers knew the riffraff they were subjecting their children to. He peered around the tiled corner, not sure who he was looking for. Cowboy took a step into the crowd then felt a pull on the back of his shirt. When he attempted to shrug it off, he felt a pinch in his neck and fell to knees.

The tile floor darkened, and Cowboy slid backward. His head smacked against the wall, somehow his body got propped up in a corner.

"What the hell?" he slurred.

"Where is Jacko?" A face appeared in front of Cowboy. This angry face pointed at Cowboy. The man's bleary finger shifted out of focus before the rest of his hand reached out and grabbed his neck.

"Who is Jacko?" he slurred.

"Jacko. He was traveling with your friends in the Beemer."

"I don't know where the Asshole is," Cowboy managed to choke out.

"I don't believe you," the face hissed. "Where's the list?"

"What list? Look, dude, I have no clue what you are talking about." Cowboy's head spun as he tried to get a clear view of the person asking questions.

"Does the girl know?" The face became only bad breath and sharp teeth.

"What, girl?" A hard slap snapped against Cowboy's cheek. "Rina? No. She's looking too." Cowboy fought to regain consciousness. The cold tile floor brought his body back to life, and

Cowboy started swinging his arms in all directions until he connected with someone's face.

"Son of a…" he heard a male cry. Cowboy's head was shoved against the titled wall. "Now you listen," although Cowboy couldn't make out a face, he knew the metallic breath of someone high on PCP. "I want my list and the other stuff that Jacko promised, got that?" Cowboy's head jerked back as a substantial force connected with his jaw. Then he heard laughter.

"Hey, boss, what about…" Cowboy heard a slap.

"Don't talk about it in front of anyone. Not that this boy is going to be of help to anyone," the laughter grew louder. "Stranger things have happened."

Then the world began to fade around Cowboy. What had Doc gotten himself into this time? Cowboy's last thoughts were of Rina. *Oh, Rina, stay safe.*

The guys behind Rina folded their bodies over the backs of the empty chairs. Pungent smoke from a joint rose up and tickled her nose.

"No thanks," she politely declined for the sixth time. Between the strong smell of skunkweed and the crowd of rasta wigs, Rina was losing her mind. The joint looked appealing, but being stoned in an FBI dude's car afterward would probably not be her best decision. Plus, the weed would only make her more paranoid than she already was.

Rina jumped out of her chair every time a man in a rasta wig passed by.

"You need to mellow out, sista," the dude with the joint explained. "Everything is cool. We are at a show. The band is going to play another set. We have the good Ganga. It is all good." He sat back and took a long drag.

Rina didn't move. "Hey, after the lights go down, can you watch my stuff?"

"But where are the Doctor and Cowboy? Why aren't they here?"

"Still not sure. They may be back, but I need to use the ladies' room…" She shook her head while the smokers giggled and repeated, "Ladies room."

"The ladies room," the guy with the joint bellowed through laughter. "Why do you need that? Women don't like fart or crap." He said this with such authority, everyone within earshot either cracked up or looked too stunned to comment. Sensing he had an audience, he continued to ramble, "Think about it. Women are squatting and squeezin' and makin' that uhhhhhhh noise, it just doesn't make sense. Besides, I mean, isn't that why they are so cranky all the time?"

Rina looked up to the ceiling, searching for an escape route. She looked back at the stoners still in the fits of giggles. "If women shit, then they would be like human and nice, and you know, not bitchy." The debate continued in the background while Rina waited for her opportunity to leave. How the heck did these idiots keep engineering jobs? She wondered if instead of making people stupid, pot just made everyone socially inept.

The lights faded while the crowd erupted. Rina crouched down and hit play/record on both decks. She grabbed her little purse out of the roadie case, waved, and headed out of the aisle.

Stoner one shouted after her, "You should really wait until they start playing. Doc is going to be pissed." Rina turned, gave a toothless smile, and continued toward the tunnel. She heard through the crowd, "She must really have to go." The path to the tunnel was littered with bodies that moved to no particular beat. This made the trek more complicated. She kept her focus on the small red exit sign hovering above the entrance.

Although finding Cowboy was her priority, Rina tried to be optimistic that he met up with some friends and decided to hang in the rafters. Typical of Cowboy, he ditched her for a better situation. As pissed as she felt, what would be the point of her yelling at him when she found him? At this juncture, he'd be too stoned to understand anyway.

She twisted then turned with those around her until she stepped out of the mayhem into an open space. A uniformed officer yelled, "You can't be over here," as his arms expanded in all directions. Then Rina held out her skirt to flash her pass.

"Oh, you are okay. Go ahead," He then motioned her through, and turned away to watch the crowd. Rina stood just inside the tunnel and waited for her eyes to adjust. Red exit signs glowed in the distance as she forced herself into the dark. She glanced upward. "Dear God, please don't let the bleacher's collapse and rain hippie bodies down upon me. What a way to go that would be."

The lit silhouette of a woman's figure caught her glance. Rina pushed the door and covered her eyes. The blinding light pounded into her brain. She clung to the wall and made her way toward the single toilet, wiping the dripping tears off her cheek. Her head lay heavy in her hands.

"Crap, what do I do now?" One wall contained a full-length mirror, and although her entire self-reflected back, Rina focused on the red marks on her neck from Meth Head Biker Dude's threat. Her gentle touch revived the hurt as she rubbed the area. She rose to the sink and scrubbed her neck with liquid soap, but the rubbing motion extended the tenderness in her throat.

Rina splashed water to rinse off the soap, soaking her t-shirt. "I'm a mess," she repeated to her reflection. She scooped up clean water to splash on her face and hair and used her skirt to dry off. "Total mess…" she proclaimed.

"I am totally screwed," Rina chanted as she went into a forward bend. "I need help," she continued reaching up toward the ceiling, "and I don't know where to turn." Weston flashed into her mind, followed by the image of an open casket. "No, no, no…" she exclaimed, holding her head. "This is no good."

Shaken, Rina pushed open the door and waited for her eyes to readjust. Faint notes echoed in the distance as the crowd screamed their approval. Rina had no clue why they cheered. Instead, she moved in the opposite direction toward a sliver of light near the end of the tunnel. She skimmed one hand along the wall as she went. Voices grew louder as the light became more distinct.

Rina stopped short as she heard an otherwise innocent statement filled with malice: "Where did you find the kid?"

"I told you, man. He was like passed out on the bathroom floor..."

"He wasn't passed out. He was drugged!" Someone shouted.

"Dude, you're at a concert. Everyone's high." A crack turned a giggle into a whimper.

A chair leg scraped against the floor. "This guy is useless. Arrest him for possession, and we'll talk once he straightens up," commanded a female voice. Rina pressed into the shadows as a uniformed officer led a long haired-hippie toward her, with his hands bound behind his back. Rina held her breath, afraid to move.

"Dude, this is bogus," the kid kept pleading his case. "That dude in the bathroom would have died if it wasn't for me."

The cop almost sounded sympathetic. "Yeah, unfortunately for you, you found the wrong dude." Rina watched the uniformed man lead the hippie out toward where Weston left his car.

"What do you think?" asked the woman's voice, which sounded familiar to Rina, demanded the focus of the room. Rina searched her memory for a face to match the voice.

"I don't know. The kid could be lying or stoned, or he could just be foolish," said a deep male voice.

"Moon is being taken to Washington General. We will have him in a safe room. The toxicology report should be here before the end of the show," the woman instructed. Rina wondered if Weston was in the room, but she didn't dare peek around the corner.

"He'll come up positive for THC."

"After tonight, we all will. It is hard not to in here," chimed in a third voice. Rina figured there are at least three people in the room, and none sounded like Weston. "We'd all probably test positive just from breathing in the air here." A round of laughter followed.

"He's not known to do anything stronger, not even alcohol," added the baritone. "The other guy, Bruce I think his name is, told us that he may be stoned when we find him but that's about it. He just stressed the importance of finding Moon."

"So we found him, now what boss?"

"We need to let Weston know about what just happened," the woman instructed. "But be careful with the rest of the information. We need to keep this quiet."

Rina froze. Whoever these guys were, they were holding Doc and now had Cowboy. She turned and as quiet as possible, made her way back through the dark into the concert hall.

I need to get my stuff and get the heck out of here, she repeated to herself. Rina made her way toward the aisle and found, amongst the swirling hippie rainbow colors, a cold pair of black eyes. Though the rasta wig sat on his lap, exposing his shaved head, there was no mistaking Meth Head Biker Dude. As in a B horror flick, Meth Head Biker Dude broke into a sadistic grin and ran his finger over his throat.

"Now my life is officially a bad cliché," Rina blurted out loud as her legs collapsed beneath her. As she fell, the scary dude disappeared, and Rina was buried in swirling skirts, unshaven legs, and Birkenstock sandals.

"Miss, are you okay?" called a uniform from the exit tunnel.

"No. Yes. I think so."

"Well, you can't stay here," he said, taking her hand and pulling her to a standing position. "You need to move. This could be a fire hazard." Rina forced a smile and glided through the crowd. She looked over both shoulders, but Meth Head Biker Dude was nowhere to be found.

A twittering lanky body slammed into hers. "Luna!" Rina exclaimed as arms flew around her neck.

"Rina, my love," Luna answered, placing a kiss on her cheek. Her long wavy hair surrounded Rina. "Where have you been?"

Rina started to cry as Luna rubbed her shoulders. "It's okay, love," she cooed. "It is all gonna be alright."

"You don't understand…" Rina took in a deep breath, "Doc and Cowboy…" she sputtered as she attempted to stop her tears. "They disappeared and now…. I'm…"

"Rina honey, breathe." Luna pulled Rina into the mouth of the tunnel. "Everything is going to be ok. Where are Doc and Cowboy?"

"I don't know," she replied with a shaky whisper as she watched Rasta wigs swirl amongst the dancers in front of her. Luna's long arms held her up as they stepped back further into the dark. With a deep breath, Rina added, "They both disappeared on me, and now I'm stuck here by myself." She gulped back tears and tried to keep her composure.

Luna waited for a beat. "You can always hang with us. You know the bus is cramped, but…" Rina shook her head and hunched forward over her cramping stomach. As much as she wanted to go with Luna, Rina knew to listen to her gut. "Do you know where they went?"

Rina hesitated, "If I knew that… I don't know anything except…" Her voice trailed off.

"Except what?" Rina looked back at Luna and shivered.

"I just needed a hug," Rina forced a smile out. "You know. Here I am, feeling sorry for myself because the guys are probably backstage having a better time." Luna smiled back and remained quiet.

"It is all good," Rina added, separating the two, "I'll meet up with you in the lot later or tomorrow. Save me some of your secret mixes!"

With that, Luna spun off into the crowd, and Rina's eyes followed her until the rainbow colors swirled together. She jumped into the dancer's pit, moving her body in opposite directions, trying to avoid the others in the crowd. Unfortunately, her timing was out of whack, and Rina kept bumping into people. "Excuse me…I'm sorry…"

She shimmied across the aisle to where the equipment sat and proceeded to break the number one rule of tapers: She packed up the gear before the encore. She threw Cowboy's tape deck into the backpack and scrunched up bundles of wires until it more or less fit. She'd rather risk the lecture on taking proper care of the equipment than stay there another minute. She placed her tape deck into the roadie case, slammed the lid, and locked the case.

"Ooooo, Doc's going to be pissed," one of the idiots called from behind. Rina folded the microphone stands and tossed the microphones into Cowboy's backpack.

"Hey Rina, doesn't Cowboy have cases for those? You know they are wicked expensive…"

"Pay attention to your own stuff, okay?" Rina barked.

"Excuse us for trying to save your ass from Doc's wrath…"

Rina whipped around to comment and found Weston standing in the doorway of the tunnel. "Idiots," she mumbled under her breath. As the house lights went up, she hiked the backpack over her shoulder, grabbed the roadie case, and tried to wriggle through the maze of equipment.

"Yo, Rina, where's your boyfriend?" one of Doc's friends, Jetter, called out.

"Don't have a boyfriend," Rina retorted, lifting the mic stand up to avoid hitting someone's head. Cowboy's bag slipped off her shoulder onto the nearest chair. She breathed deep.

"Come on, Rina, I am just busting you. Actually, I have been looking for the Doctor all night," he whined.

"Dude, he took off with the Asshole, and I haven't seen him all day." Rina let the last part slip.

"Why the heck does he hang with that dirtbag?" Jetter threw his hands up. "I mean Doc is a good guy and that dirt bag…."

"Yeah," Rina said, as she started walking away. "I'm kind of worried about him myself. But I am working on finding him."

"You need a place?" Jetter asked as he shifted his weight.

"No, thanks. I'm good," Rina said. She watched Jetter let out a long breath.

"If you see him…"

"I'll pass on that you're looking." Rina repositioned Cowboy's backpack and proceeded to hobble through the chairs. She looked up in time to catch Weston's eye and mouth "help."

Rina wriggled through the crowd to Weston and dropped the gear at his feet.

"Yeah, thanks for your help," she spat out. Rina spun around to follow Weston's eyes around the emptying-coliseum. She scanned the floor along with any other areas she could see from her angle. A long breath escaped when Meth Head Biker Dude failed to appear. Though a few folks lingered on the upper levels, she couldn't make them out, and her stomach settled.

"Did you hear me?"

"I didn't realize you needed help," he commented. His lips turned upward into a smile. Rina's pulse quickened and slowed. Maybe I should have gone with Jetter, she thought. A night locked in a hotel bathroom had to be better than this. "Are you ok?" Weston asked.

"Oh, sure."

"Well, you had a weird expression on your face, like you unconsciously left the building or something." Rina shrugged. "What's with the new backpack?"

"It's my friend Cowboy's," Rina answered.

"Who?"

"The Cowboy. He is a friend of Doc's and mine." Weston took the roadie case from Rina and grabbed the mic stands. He went to reach for the backpack as she turned up toward him. Their faces were so close she could feel his breath. "He disappeared during the show," she whispered.

Weston nodded and stood. Though buried under her gear, he managed a free hand to help Rina off the floor. He led her down the now well-lit tunnel toward the room where Rina had overheard. Cowboy was in the hospital. As they approached the area, her stomach flipped.

"Huh?"

"The concert. How was it?"

"Nerve-wracking…"

"Nerve-wracking? Why?" Rina followed Weston around the corner. Over in the distance, she swore she saw Meth Head Biker Dude hanging out with a bunch of uniformed police. They looked to be laughing.

"Hey," Rina stopped and grabbed Weston's arm. She turned to point back at the group, only to find Meth Head Biker Dude had disappeared.

"What?"

Rina shook her head and stared for a minute. "Nothing. I thought I saw someone I knew." She moved toward the parking area. Once the gear was loaded in the back, Rina jumped in the passenger's seat and locked the door. Weston watched her fold her arms, hugging herself. "I want to go home," she stated.

"We are going home," Weston answered. "Unless you are hungry. I know this great all-night diner…"

"No. I want to go back to Connecticut. Skip the next show." She winced then added, "I just want to go home and for my life to be normal again."

Weston stared out into the traffic. His hands squeezed and released the steering wheel.

"Did you hear me? I want to go home!" Rina's voice pitched upward.

"Yeah, I heard you," he sighed. "Look, Rina, we need to talk about that when we get back to my place."

"Talk about what?" Her knee bounced on the leather. "I don't think we have anything to talk about. I actually think all you need to do is drop me at Washington National, and I can figure it out from there. I can take the red-eye back. My car is already at the airport, and I'll just call work to say I am back early and ready to pick up a few extra shifts. Then all will be good." Rina looked out the window as they passed the all night basketball leagues. "We are not heading towards the airport, are we?"

"No."

"But..."

"Rina, for once in your life, I need you to be patient. Can you do that?" Weston's voice rose in the silence.

Rina turned her focus and her body toward the window. She watched the tree-lined neighborhood pass by. Her face became wet, but she refused to reach up to wipe her cheek. Weston looked over and shook his head. Some things hadn't changed about Rina. His old frustrations began to surface.

How long will this one last, he wondered? When they were dating, Rina was always getting pissed off about something minor. When he'd be late to pick her up or didn't call after an away game. Sometimes something just popped in her head. She wouldn't say what she was upset about, but would just go off on these non-speaking tangents. Then out of nowhere, everything would be fine and dandy. She would start talking to him again, like nothing happened. He never could figure this characteristic out, although Rina wasn't the only female he had encountered who had this habit.

Weston pulled the car into his space, and before he cut the engine, Rina had the back door open. She grabbed her roadie case, walked over to the elevator, and stood with her back to him, tapping her feet. Weston grabbed the rest of the gear, slid past, and entered.

Rina glanced over to see Cowboy's backpack secure on Weston's shoulder. She shook her head, thinking Weston would want to search Cowboy's pack first, then arrest her for his weed. Inside the doorway, Rina proceeded to stomp her way up the stairs.

Sitting on the kitchen counter, Weston heard the shower turn on upstairs. He opened up his computer and waited for the screen to warm up. Sooner or later, he would have to go up and explain to her why she couldn't leave. Though he

knew she deserved an explanation, he was
determined to put it off as long as possible.

Rina dropped the roadie case on the bed and ripped her shirt over her head. She tossed it next to her backpack then removed her skirt, bra, and underwear. The bathroom floor warmed her feet as she strolled naked toward the big shower. She reached inside and turned the water on hot. Once the room had steamed, she stepped under the rain flow showerhead and allowed the warmth to hug her entire body. Eyes shut, Rina pictured being outside the car, waiting for Doc after a show. The steady beat of the rain brought back flashes of Saratoga, Hershey Park, and Red Rocks—all beautiful outdoor venues that the band rocked while it rained so hard.

She wished her and Doc had gone back to the Greek in Berkley instead of doing another east coast swing. Maybe the Asshole wouldn't have traveled with them since flying was involved. Perhaps he would have gotten busted on his own, and she would have seen him on the news, as another junkie who deserved his sentence. Doc is a good friend, one who she loved to be around, and who looked out for her.

Rina wanted to help Doc because he would do the same for her. Weston's face flashed in front of her, and just as quick, she pictured Meth Head Biker Dude. The two images morphed together and then apart. Rina shook her head, both disintegrated like an Etch-A-Sketch drawing.

As the water started to cool, Rina washed from head to toe, then toweled off and combed out her hair. She tied a towel around her midsection and walked out of the bathroom to find Weston sitting on the bed. Rina showed neither surprise nor shock by his presence.

"Thought this was my space," she commented.

"It is," Weston replied. He stared at the light blue towel covering her. Rina followed his eyes and laughed.

"Keep on dreaming, buddy."

"Been there, seen that," Weston said while he diverted his gaze. "Besides as tempting as you are right now, we need to talk about what happened at the show."

"Why, what happened at the show," Rina turned and asked. She rummaged through her backpack, finally pulling out a crinkled tie-dyed sundress. With one move, she draped the dress over her body and let the towel drop to the floor.

As the dress flowed around her body, Weston's eyes clung to her breasts.

"Hey, do you have a washer? Because I was going to do laundry at the hotel, but as you can see, I am not there."

Still staring at the towel on the floor, Weston said, "That was the sexist thing I have ever seen you do."

Rina shot back a look. She plopped down on the floor opposite Weston and crossed her legs for effect. She leaned against the opposite wall, putting as much space between her Weston as possible.

"So what about the show?" she asked.

"I asked you first."

"Wes, I am so tired. Do we have to play this game?" she whined. "I think I just want to call an airline and fly home. This tour is a bust."

"You can't do that." Weston stared into her eyes. When Rina mirrored the same look to his challenge, something from the past stirred up. Though the two could sit like this for hours, Wes usually gave in.

"Why not?"

"Tangy, tell me about tonight's show."

"Tell me why I can't go home," she replied. Rina switched her legs around as Weston sighed. "And don't call my Tangy."

Weston began folding then refolding his arms. Hard lines stood out across his jaw. The staring contest brought the conversation to a standstill.

"You know I am kind of pissed," Rina started. "Why did you put me in this situation in the first place? My friends are getting hurt. I can't go home. And of all my ex's, you had to be the one to come back into my life." She watched Weston raise his eyebrow. "There weren't that many," she assured with a smirk. "But seriously. I mean, really, why? Why me?" She breathed in deep and exhaled with a loud swish. Weston didn't say anything. He had a job to do. Rina should be weeping in his arms, grateful to be safe. She should tell him about what happened. He shouldn't have to beg.

"Say something!" Rina screamed.

"Okay."

"Okay, what?"

"Okay, let's talk. I'll ask you a question then after you answer you get to ask me one. We go back and forth until we are both satisfied. Fair?"

"Ah, tit for tat."

"Yeah, something like that," Weston replied, his eyes dark and sexy.

"I get to go first..." Before Rina responded, he held his hands out to stop her. "Did anything happen at the show tonight?"

"Doc is missing, so I had to do the flips. Now it is my turn."

"No. Come on, Tangy, er, I mean Rina. I am trying to help you."

"Point taken. We have Cowboy's backpack because he took off and never came back…" Rina brought her index finger to her mouth and started to chew a nail.

"Where was he going?"

"Hey, what about my question?"

"You are right. Please proceed."

"Do you know where Cowboy is?"

"Mr. Moon is under heavy guard at the hospital. He almost OD-ed."

"That can't be right. Cowboy doesn't do drugs."

"Really, Rina?"

"Okay, so he smokes a little pot, but in all our years of traveling together, I have never seen him do anything stronger. The dude doesn't even drink! I'm telling you, that is not the Cowboy."

"That is interesting because your boy had so many pharmaceuticals in him, he could have opened a drug store."

"Are you sure it was Cowboy?"

"The dude you were sitting with before the show, preppy shirt, slick hair?" Rina's eyes grew wide as she nodded. So Weston had been watching her. "Then it was the Cowboy. Don't you know anyone's actual name?" Rina gave a shrug. Weston watched her eyes begin to water. Without a thought, he added, "I can try to get you in to see him tomorrow."

"Really?"

"Yes. I can try. That way, we will both be sure who he is."

"That would be great." In a whisper, she added, "Thank you."

"So: what was Cowboy doing?"

"He went to find out information about Doc, well actually the Asshole, so we could figure out the Doc situation. I am not sure who he went looking for."

"Good to know, thank you." Weston waited then gestured your turn.

"Is Cowboy going to be ok?"

"We hope so. Rina, how did he know about the Doc situation?"

"Oh no," Rina replied, waving her finger. "My turn. Why can't I go home tomorrow?"

"Because this situation will not go away, and here I can keep you safe."

"What situation?"

"No fair my turn," Weston interrupted.

"Hey, you didn't answer my question! What is this?" Rina asked, putting this in air quotes, a gesture she despised since her boss at the casino used them far too much.

"The reason you are not in a jail cell next to Doc," Weston said as Rina's eyes widened, "is because I said I would keep an eye on you. Otherwise, you would be looking for a lawyer too."

"Do I need a lawyer?" Rina leaned forward.

"Not at this point, however, the possibility still exists."

"Huh?" She sat back and let the silence take over. Rina looked up and pointed at Weston, opened her mouth, then dropped her hands back in her lap. After a few rotations, she finally managed to say, "So Doc's in jail?"

"He is for now."

"Can I see him?" Weston's face relaxed.

"Maybe."

"Maybe?"

"I will see what I can do," he hesitated before continuing, "Tangy, here I can keep you safe. If you decide you really want to leave, I can't stop you, but I also can't guarantee you or your family's safety or that you wouldn't be arrested."

"Arrested for what? I didn't do anything!"

"Yeah, you did." Weston paused, then added, "Drug trafficking."

"Are you insane?" Rina stood to stretch. As she moved toward the window, her dress became sheer, showing the silhouette of her body. Weston's groan had her turn, revealing even more. "I didn't know what they were doing," she started to say. "I just thought the guy was an asshole that Doc was giving a lift to. I didn't even like hanging out with the slimebag." Rina shook her head and stared up at the skylight. "I really had no idea what Doc was doing besides giving the jerk a ride." Rina threw her arm`s up in the air as she spoke. The dress flew around, giving Weston glimpses of her actual flesh.

"Rina, you have got to understand the FBI's point of view…"

"Well, I don't," she barked and wrapped her arms around her shaking body. "I don't have to understand anything. I mean, really, I guess I am just screwed. One friend is in jail. Another is in a hospital bed. I got Meth Head Biker Dude following me around, threatening my wellbeing plus just general strangeness happening everywhere. On top of all that, I feel petrified, and I am so hungry."

Weston stood to bring Rina into his arms. The warmth of his touch was no match for the pounding of her heart. Weston tightened his hold while Rina leaned in, too weak to raise her arms. He stroked her back, then whispered, "Tangy, what did you just say?"

"I'm hungry," she quivered in return.

"I'll order you a pizza. Now please repeat what you just said."

Rina leaned into his chest and mumbled something that sounded like, "Meth Head Biker Dude."

"Okay. What or who is a Meth Head Biker Dude?" Rina's body quaked as Weston pulled back. Rina stared in the direction of the braided rug. She concentrated on the floor then hit his chin as she looked back up.

"Why is it so clean up here? I mean, no dust bunnies?" Weston pulled her back into a tight hug. Her arms hung straight by her side, but Rina allowed her head to return to the warm spot against his chest. Weston moved his hands up and down her shivering back.

"Tangy, it is going to be ok," he murmured. "You just have to let me in and tell me what is going on." As he looked into her eyes, he begged, "Come on, Rina, you know you can tell me anything. You always at least trusted me..."

Rina brought her arms around Weston's waist and squeezed. Weston manipulated both bodies on to the end of the bed, so they could sit rather than stand. He brushed her wet hair off her face, then again raised her chin. He looked down to see the dress wet, clinging, and revealing everything it covered.

"It is okay, Tangy. I am going to protect you," Weston whispered in between her sobs. His hand still circled around her soaked back. "I'm going to take care of you." He held on to her shaking body and waited.

Rina looked straight into Weston's eyes. Although the voices inside her head whispered to beware, he displayed concern for her wellbeing, so Rina barely touched her lips to Weston's. Eyes wide open, he looked back at her, and Rina knew that look.

"I'm fine," she stated, sliding away. "Everything is…just fine."

"No, you are not," Weston said as Rina slid further away. Weston shut his eyes, waiting for her to talk. He lay down against the pillow, and Rina followed suit. She angled her body away, but her head managed to find the nook in his shoulder snuggle in to. Weston reached over and took her hand in his.

Rina waited for Weston to stroke her hair, a sure sign he was willing to take advantage of the situation, but he rubbed his thumb against her hand. The two sides lay in the safe spot between their bodies.

Rina sighed loud and moved her head onto another pillow without letting go of Weston's hand.

Weston held Rina's warm body against his, fighting to stay awake. He waited until her breath became rhythmic then slipped out of bed. He placed a blanket over her body and watched her sleep for a minute, noting how angelic she looked when she wasn't complaining.

Weston went down to the kitchen and heated water for tea. He checked his computer for Mary's summary of the night's activities. Weston had spent most of the evening overseeing the operation from the monitor room. From his view, several inconsistencies went along with the reports his team had filed so far. Not for the first time, he wondered if his rogue agent had convinced others to join him.

He poured the hot water into a mug and added a decaf green tea bag along with a teaspoon of local honey to help with his allergies. Weston sat and scrolled through each agent's wrap up, stopping when he got to Beman's:

"Agent Marconi, Wilson, and I proceeded to follow Moon to the top level of the building where we immediately lost him in-crowd. Agent Wilson was summoned by a concertgoer about a half-hour later who reported a man passed out in the men's room. Emergency personal removed the person later identified as Moon. There was no other information as of yet on what caused him to pass out, although the EMTs believed it to be from illegal substances. The person who found him was questioned and arrested for possession. No other information is available at this time. Moon was transferred to a local hospital and is under guard."

Weston sat back and sighed. He glanced at the report from the other two involved. Nothing more stood out, yet something was off. It was after two in the morning, yet he still picked up the phone.

"Who is guarding Moon?" Weston barked into the receiver.

"Good morning to you too, boss," Mary responded.

"I knew you'd still be up too, Mary. And I apologize for the abruptness." Weston sighed. "I just want to make sure…"

"I got the boys from the FBI out there along with Wilson, why?"

"Pull Wilson and put him on finding who did this. There is no reason to have a narcotics expert playing babysitter."

"I thought it would make sense since he was one of the guys to find him," Weston looked back at Wilson's report. Nothing about finding Moon was mentioned. Mary continued, "I also thought you wanted our guys to handle everything because of the internal issues. Did I miss something?"

"No, Mary, you did fine. I would rather have Wilson keep searching since he is really good at finding leads."

"Do I need to get another babysitter for Moon?"

"No, Mary. I'll take care of it. Just get some rest. We got a lot to do tomorrow."

"Gotcha boss. You need rest too. Get some sleep." Weston stared at Mary's evening summary then sighed.

"You got it. Thanks for picking up." Weston disconnected and continued reading. His tea had gone cold, yet he didn't notice. The words on the screen bothered him. Her summary missed the essential details that he had witnessed on the monitors. There also appeared to be conflicting information about who actually found Moon in the men's room. Reaching over, he dialed another familiar number and waited.

"I need your help," he stated. The voice on the other end started sleepy yet became clearer as Weston proceeded to read the night's summary along with the various individual reports.

"Do you think she's involved?" Marty Richards asked. Marty worked in the DEA and was considered to be up there in the organization. It was Marty who discovered the original leak in Weston's ranks. The two were distant cousins and knew each other since birth as they shared the same date. They also served together for a brief time in Iraq. Weston only bothered Marty with the big stuff, and this seemed to be getting bigger by the minute.

"I'm not sure. I want to say no, but the evidence says otherwise."

"And you are certain that it wasn't an oversight?"

"Yes."

"Okay, then. What do you need from me?"

"A guard for Moon over at the hospital is a must. Make it someone who wouldn't draw suspicion. I don't know. Do you have anyone on your team that you can spare who could help with the investigation?"

"Let me think about it later. I'll get the hospital taken care of when we hang up." After a pause, Marty asked, "When do you think I can start doing the pick-ups? I'd like to get this whole mess taken care of quick."

"Me too, Marty. What do you think? I don't want to set off any alarms in their organization. So far, Jacko has told us nothing, and the other guy either doesn't know anything or is an outstanding actor."

"What about the girl? You know, screensaver?"

Weston wished he hadn't shared his connection to Rina. He didn't think she was involved, but his gut said, leaving her on her own would be dangerous. Choosing his words carefully, Weston answered, "I am not sure yet. I think she's not involved…"

"Then cut her loose. You don't need the distraction."

"I know, but I think she could help still since the others think she knows something."

"Does she have the distribution list?"

"Not that she knows of, or that I can find, yet as I mentioned the whole bait angle…"

"Bait, huh? Not sure that is a good plan. You still have emotions there."

"Not anymore. Besides, I can do this, Marty. No individual rides above the team, remember?"

"Yeah, I remember. I'll take care of the hospital. Give a call back when you've got more, and in the meantime, I'll see about looking into phone records, etc."

"Sounds good. Thanks, Marty." Weston hung up the phone as his computer slipped into sleep mode. The photo of him and Rina at the beach popped up on his screensaver. He reached out to stroked Rina's cheek with his finger.

Damn, he had it bad. Weston thought about what Marty had said. The whole investigation was getting out of control, and in the past week, he had too many team members go from asset to suspect. Ever since he picked up Jacko, things had gotten more heated.

Weston clicked off his computer. At least this Bruce character and Jacko were in safe places. He was smart enough to transfer both to Marty's holding tank, along with Lyle Tremont, the other suspect they arrested in that bust. Although several people, including Beman and Mary, had inquired to their whereabouts, Weston only reported that since they were part of an east coast trafficking crackdown, they now were custody of Customs.

The move made sense, and he knew that no one in his department wanted to venture over to question the Customs department. He hoped that they looked at both suspects as write-offs. It helped that drug control had become the family business. His cousin Marty was the liaison between his department and the DEA. Weston had his department within the FBI, and both couldn't operate without Uncle Sal in Customs.

The best part was very few knew of the tie between the men, and the men kept the connection secret. That may have to change after this, Weston thought.

Sunlight streamed through the skylights to warm the room. Rina fought with the blanket covering her legs until she rolled to freedom. Blurry eyed, she focused on her surroundings. Still, in her gauze dress, she lay sideways across the bed. The blankets piled in all in different directions looked like someone had break danced on the bed. Weston was nowhere nearby.

Rina stretched her arms over her head, then rolled her body into a sitting position. A long growl escaped from her stomach, but the shower beckoned first. The warm spray woke the rest of her body. After a few stretches, she dried off and dressed fast, pulling out a mini skirt and t-shirt from her backpack.

Weston's bed on the second-floor landing lay perfect, made up while all the clothes put away. He must have a fairy housecleaner, Rina giggled. She wandered down the second set of stairs toward the kitchen.

Weston perched on a barstool drinking out of a coffee mug. He concentrated on the open file in front of him. "Coffee in the pot," he gestured to the counter, without looking away from his work.

"Don't do coffee," Rina answer as she proceeded to open and close each cabinet door.

"You are almost there," Weston answered at the same moment, Rina reached up for a glass. She walked over to the refrigerator for ice and water. Opening the door, it was not surprising to find the hollow space near empty. A container of nonfat milk along with a few bottles of mustard lined the top shelf. In contrast, a smattering of takeout containers spread across the others.

"You're a nutritious eater," Rina commented. Even though Weston appeared to be concentrating on the papers on the counter, Rina could feel his every move. It was a similar sensation to when they sat in the same math class on opposite sides of the room. She would feel that jolt, turn, and see Weston wink in her direction. Or Rina would be walking by herself down an empty hallway, and just as she smiled, Weston would magically appear in front of her.

She could feel those little reminders while she did the simple task of filling her water glass. This is why Weston was unique to her. Rina turned to watch Weston engrossed in his papers as she sipped the ice-cold water. She moved around to his side, attempting to sneak a glance at what was so interesting. Weston turned ever so slightly to block her view.

"Got any real food?"

"Oranges in the bowl. There may be some leftover takeout in the fridge."

Rina returned to the refrigerator and proceeded to inspect the takeout. "How old is this?"

"It's still good," Weston answered without looking up. She dropped the substance into the trash and proceeded to open another Styrofoam surprise. Even if it looked good, it smelled terrible. She dumped the unidentifiable plié of brown mush, and then a container of wilted lettuce decomposing into more mush. Rina didn't bother to open the last box. She just threw it out.

"Do you have anything edible? Those were disgusting. I mean, how long had those containers been in there?"

"I don't know. Maybe a couple days?" Weston glanced up to see Rina giving him the stare down. "Okay, maybe longer. Whatever. There are takeout menus in the drawer to your left. Find something and order it. They all deliver."

"I saw a market down the street. I think I'll just take a walk and… What?" Weston returned the stare down.

"I'll go with you," he replied, putting the file back into his briefcase.

"That's okay. I don't want to keep you from working…" They went back to the staring contest. Rina's heart sped up, then slowed. She took a step closer to Weston, and then backed up against the counter. Her head made one decision while her body went back into high school mode. He still had that pull. The heart wanted to be held. Her body wanted more, yet the conditions were all wrong. She shook her head.

"Can I go see Cowboy?" she asked, breaking the mind-body Ping-Pong match. "Maybe get some food along the way?" Again Weston showed nothing but the stare down. Rina slammed her glass into the sink a little harder than expected. "Or I can just stay here and rot!" The air conditioner ticked on breaking into the stillness. Neither party moved.

Rina turned to stomp back up the stairs. She would rather pout by herself then sulk in front of another person. She got halfway to the second floor when Weston finally answered, "Okay, we will go get food, then we can swing by the hospital."

"For real?" Rina started back down the stairs.

"For real and bring your ticket and stuff in case we don't get back here…"

"I'm not going to another show."

"Tangy."

"Don't call me that." Another staredown began. Weston let out a long sigh.

"We have been over this. You have to go because if you don't go or you try to go home…"

"I know — you will arrest me." She replied with an exaggerated eye roll.

Weston nodded. "Please do this for me. I know I'm asking a lot, but I really need you to do this." Weston sucked in a deep breath. "It's the only way I can keep you safe."

"Safe," Rina did another eye roll, threw her hands up, and then headed up to the third floor to grab her stuff.

Weston watched her go. He reached down to grab the file and stared at the first page again. Rina smiled back at him from the photo taken at Saratoga. He let out a long sigh.

He couldn't let his emotions take over him like this, but holding her last night brought back a nearness he hadn't felt in ages.

If only they had lasted.

Rina slumped down, arms crossed in the passenger's seat while Weston took back roads through the city. In the middle of a quiet neighborhood, he pulled next to what was once a KFC.

"I don't eat junk food," Rina stated.

"I know," Weston replied as he inched toward the speaker. Rina sat up and read the sign: Zen Master Jam Vegetarian.

"This is so cool," she strained to read the menu. "Drive-thru vegetarian. Ok. I want the organic blueberry muffin infused with protein and an iced green tea with honey, please." She squinted to read the specials on the other side. "Oh, and can I have an order of veggie sausage, too?" Weston turned to smile in her direction as she shrugged. "I need extra protein for all the stress you are causing me." That brought out a laugh. He could still measure the scope of how upset she was by the size of her sandwich. The larger the lunch, the worse his day would be.

Weston repeated the order and shoed away the money she offered.

"You are not eating?"

"I already ate," he replied as he watched Rina break off pieces of the muffin and stuff the bits into her mouth. She offered him a taste. "No, thanks. Health food can kill you," he laughed.

"Yeah, and the three-day-old pizza from your fridge is the most nutritious meal ever." Rina brought her attention back to her food, then reclined back to sip the refreshing sweet tea.

Another couple of turns and they pulled into another common underground parking area. Weston stopped, flashed his ID, found a parking space then started to instruct, "Tangy, you must stay close to me here." Rina nodded. "I'm serious. This is a secure facility and any wandering…"

"Got it," she saluted as he trotted towards the elevator. They got off into a lobby area with a security desk buzzing people through a metal detector. The walls, couches, floors, and tables were all shiny, clean, and white.

Again, Weston flashed his ID and said something to the guard Rina couldn't hear. The guard looked back at her, nodded, and buzzed them both through.

Past the main door, the bland décor was broken up with dozens of plaques along the wall. Rina stopped to read the one dedicated to

President Eisenhower. As she stared at the wording, someone tugged on her arm. Weston was pulling her away while sporting an *Are you kidding me* expression.

"Stay close to me," he whispered through his clenched jaw.

Weston continued to flash his ID, and besides the occasional head nod to indicate Rina was with him, he said nothing. In silence, they rode the elevator up three floors.

The doors opened to a six-foot-plus giant in black suit pants, a white button-down shirt, an American flag tie, and Glock attached to his belt. One hand rested on the gun while he blocked the entrance to the floor. His eyes met Weston's then quickly scanned the ID. Both men wore no expression.

"Her too?" the guard head nodded toward Rina.

"Yes," Weston replied. The guard moved to one side, saluted Weston, and then went back into position. Rina shivered. She followed Weston down the plain white hall to another door where a similar routine took place.

The room had no lights, although a little brightness appeared from behind a window on the opposite wall. As Rina moved towards the glass, a gasp escaped from her lips. The lifeless body covered in tubes was her friend Cowboy. The tubes and wires hooked up to machines, which surrounded the room in blinking lights. She couldn't hear any sounds although she sensed there had to be beeps. Cowboy laid still, eyes closed, and Rina watched as his chest moved up and down with each breath. His body moved to the mysterious rhythm that his head often moved to.

"Can I go in?" Rina whispered. She stood as though any wrong movement would cause something terrible to happen.

Weston hesitated. "Wait here," he instructed and left the room. A tear moved down Rina's cheek as she whispered, "This is entirely my fault, I should have told him Doc was sick at the hotel." Watching the lights blinking, Rina calmed herself by forcing her breath into the same rhythm as Cowboy. Her face stayed wet, yet her heart slowed. Small bumps formed on her exposed skin. She started to rub her biceps for warmth.

The door clicked open, and Rina jumped. Weston returned with some guy in a white lab coat. "Please do not touch any of the machines," he instructed as he handed Rina a similar jacket to put on. "And please do not disturb the patient." She followed him through a glass door in the corner of the room.

A toxic, sterile stench filled the air, and Rina covered her mouth to keep from retching. Lysol on steroids popped into her brain.

"You'll get used to that after a minute," the lab coat indicated.

Rina looked back to see Weston's shadow in the glass. It could have been anybody, looking through the one-way lens, but the warmth from his gaze gave her a feeling of comfort. His presence comforted Rina yet alarmed her at the same time.

The man in the lab coat man moved Cowboy to a sitting position. His eyes closed, that grin plastered on his face usually meant trouble for Rina. Cowboy glowed. Rina shivered.

"Can he hear me?" Lab coat man nodded. Rina sat in the only chair next to the bed. She reached out to hold Cowboy's hand and was relieved his touch was warm.

"Hey now, Cowboy." Rina felt a little squeeze of her fingers. Her eyes started to water again. "It is Rina. I was actually worried about you," she tried to laugh but ended up coughing back a tear. When Cowboy squeezed a second time, one of the beeps went at a faster pace. This caught the attention of lab tech who walked over and pretended to adjust the machine.

Rina looked back at the glass and saw a second shadow next to Wes. She tried to get a face yet only saw the outline. A nurse entered the room and proceeded to fuss with the wiring, like the waitress who cleaned nonexistent crumbs off the table near a good-looking guy. The nurse fiddled with the wires and fluffed the blankets, yet stayed away from Rina.

"You missed a crappy show," Rina started saying. She thought Cowboy's smile widened a little. "And a lot of folks came by looking for you. By the way, I packed up all your stuff and took it with me." That got another squeeze. "The idiots behind us kept coming by looking for you, busting me about getting the flips right..." Cowboy rubbed Rina's hand with his thumb. The movement so gentle, she barely noticed. "I did get the flips by the way, not that I want to do them all the time. Paying attention during a show takes too much headspace for me."

She watched Cowboy's thumb make a small gentle circle on her hand. "I did start the second set early because I needed to use the lady's room, other than that things went smooth." Rina moved her thumb in the opposite direction of Cowboy's. Her voice became more stage, less whisper. "Those guys behind us are complete idiots, by the way. You should have heard them." At the mention of Doc's name Cowboy gave a little squeeze.

"Rina," Weston appeared at her side. "Sorry, it is time to go."

Rina ignored Wes and kept her focus on Cowboy. "I'll try to come back to see you again," her voice became quieter. She leaned over to give Cowboy a kiss and a soft hug. "We will get these guys," she promised as Cowboy moved his head to the side, and the beeping noise increased.

Rina let go of his hand, turned, and walked straight into the hallway. She stood erect and waited for Weston to follow. The guard gave Rina the staredown, so she caught his eyes and rolled hers. The man actually broke protocol and smiled.

Weston arrived. Rina followed close as they walked back through the maze. Not one person stopped to check Weston's ID, yet many saluted as he passed. Neither said a word until they turn up back at Weston's car.

"Thank you," Rina whispered.

"You are welcome." Weston stared straight ahead. She wanted him to ask for details about her visit. She wanted him to tell her everything would be okay, and he had the situation under control. If ever there was a time to BS her, it was now. Instead, Weston's silence settled over the air, a sign she read as proof of his callousness, and that this was all just part of his job.

Back on the street, he maneuvered through the tree-lined neighborhoods, similar to the one where they had first found each other. He slowed down as they drove passed an apartment building akin to the one where she had last seen Doc, then sped over to the main road.

Weston went back to the Zen Garden drive-thru ordering a salad with fish. This time Rina opted for a veggie burger that boasted twenty grams of protein without the roll. The smell of food permeated the car as they drove in silence back to his nondescript office building.

Back in Weston's office, Mary set out silverware, napkins, and glasses of ice water on the coffee table. She handed Weston a stack of messages along with a manila folder. Mary turned and gave a quick smile that disappeared as swiftly as it had appeared.

Weston placed the file on the table, opened it, and started eating his salad.

Rina gasped. There lay a photo of Meth Head Biker Dude sitting next to her at the concert.

"Friend of yours?" He asked in between bites. Rina sat in silence. "The photo was taken last night," he continued.

"I don't know him."

"Then why were you talking to him?"

"I wasn't," Rina shuttered. "He was... I don't know."

"Okay. Then why was he following you?"

"I don't know." Weston slid his chair closer, then rested his arm on Rina's shoulders.

"Did he threaten you?" Rina said nothing and took a forkful of veggie burger in her mouth. Instead of tasting the garlic, zucchini, spicy-black bean mixture that had permeated the car, Rina felt nothing. The burgers' texture had turned to cardboard. Another photo, taken through the crowd, showed Meth Head Biker Dude watching her enter the tunnel. The third picture proved the most disturbing.

"What the heck?" Rina spat veggie burger on the table.

"What the heck indeed," Weston commented back. He reached for the third photo that showed a clean-cut version of the same guy in an FBI ID badge. Rina gasped as the dead eyes, and thin scar confirmed her worst fears.

"Marshall Butmon. He's with you?"

"Not exactly." Rina watched Weston take another bite of salad. Her legs started to bounce with the chair. She took a deep breath, then slumped. "He was with us at one time."

Rina sat back and shook her head. "So that's how he could go anywhere. It wasn't my imagination when I saw him backstage hanging with the cops…"

"Why didn't you say something?" Weston asked in between bites.

"I really just wanted to go home. Really, I had had a full night. You know, lost a friend, visited the ladies' room, had my life threatened…

I mean, at 5'3," my bad-assed attitude wasn't going to get me too far." That got a laugh from Weston. "Plus, I didn't want to end up in the hospital like…" Rina held on to herself and waited. "I just wanted to go home," she whispered.

"Why?"

"Why? Didn't you hear me? He threatened me… and you." Weston let out a deep sigh while he stared at the photo. "Are you going to tell me about him or what?" Rina's foot started to move again.

"As of today, he is still technically employed by the FBI. Internal affairs are taking care of that," Weston stared for a minute at the photo then looked back at Rina. "He is actually part of the larger Jacko—" Weston's face broke into a grin, "I mean the Asshole investigation." His last comment didn't even render a return smile.

"Huh." Rina nodded to a silent beat. "How is he involved?"

"I can't tell you that, but I can say that he is tied to Jacko and some other nasty people." He watched Rina's leg move quicker. Weston ran his hands over his face. How he wanted to trust her yet revealing that he had someone become a double agent and there could be more involved, would only put Rina in more danger. "And we will get him off the streets as quickly as possible," he assured. Rina nodded her head, back to the beat, no one else could hear.

"So," she finally asked. Weston twirled his fork for her to continue. "I mean not to be egocentric, but what about me?"

Weston gaffed. "Yeah, no ego there." He shifted his body closer to Rina's, and then reached over to remove the crumbs that cling to her lips. Rina's body tightened and her face flushed.

"We think…"

"Who's 'we?'" Rina's question brought a massive smile to Weston's face.

"As I was saying," he continued, "We think you should talk to Doc and find out what he knows."

"I can talk to Doc?" Weston nodded. Rina took another bite of veggie burger then chewed slow. "When?"

"We think…"

"Okay, Wes," Rina held her hand up. "Stop saying 'we' unless you are going to introduce me to the others."

"That is fair enough," Weston responded with a laugh. "We would like you to see him today before the show."

"I'm not going to the show."

"Yes, you are, and you are going to tape it and act like nothing is wrong."

"I can't set up the equipment by myself…"

"Then, I will get you help."

"Yeah, but Meth Head Biker Dude…" Rina crossed her arms while rubbing her biceps. "He will know." Weston burst into laughter and wrote *Meth Head Biker Dude* in big letters on the photo from the previous evening. Rina's mouth dropped.

"Glad you think this is funny," she choked out.

"No, Rina. Finally, we have an acronym we can use." Weston ran his hand across his mouth. "The guy who is going to be with you has been on tour for a while. You might even recognize him. You need to greet him as an old friend. You know, as you people do."

"Don't say, you people…"

"You know what I mean." Rina shrugged.

"It is still insulting…"

"What would you like me to say?" Rina could see she was getting to Wes. She broke out into a big smile.

"I'm only taking my stuff in. Cowboy can get my copies."

"Fine. Do whatever. I don't care about the tapes," Rina gave him an exaggerated eye roll, "or the details. You just have to be normal. Can you do that? Just do what you do. Meth Head Biker Dude," Weston shook his head to stay composed, "will contact you again. He has been desperate since we busted the Asshole."

"What if I need help?"

"Glad you asked." Weston turned and shouted, "Mary" at the door. A small commotion could be heard coming from the direction of Mary's desk. After a beat of silence, a tall, lanky guy with out of control, curly brown hair bounced in looking like a typical hippie stereotype. He wore an old torn tie-dyed t-shirt with jean cut-offs, also full of rips, and maybe three days' worth of facial hair, not quite a beard, yet scruffy. His eyes appeared half-closed, and of course, he sported the classic stoner grin.

"Hey now," he greeted as he sprang into the room. He wrapped his arms around Rina in a tight hug, then just as quickly broke the squeeze and plopped down in the chair next to her. He reached across to help himself to the rest of her veggie burger, then sat back and grinned while chewing. "You mind?" he asked after he swallowed half of what was in his mouth.

Though the guy had a look, something still screamed authority figure. "He doesn't smell right," Rina commented. "People will know."

"Smell, right?" Weston asked. "What do you mean?"

"Actually, I just got what they mean by 'smells like a narc,'" Rina held her hands in front. "No offense."

"None taken," the false hippie answered, now sitting up straight at attention. "By the way, I am Conrad Beman, the third," he extended his hand, which Rina shook. "But, you should call me Wayback."

"Wayback?"

"Yes, Wayback. That is my tour name because whenever someone asks how I know the dude I'm hanging with, I always answer we go way back."

"What?"

"It just works. Folks see me as a trust fund kid whose funds are still going," he laughed. "Know what I mean?"

Rina giggled along then introduced herself although she knew he knew who she was. "You still smell too good," she added, "even for a trustafarian."

Wayback leaned over, and in a stage whisper said, "I know of a way we could take care of that," then, while Rina blushed, he turned to Weston, adding, "Dude, she is gorgeous! How did you ever blow this one?" He jerked his thumb towards Rina.

Weston ignored the comment. "Okay, you two need to meet up on the floor, but not before the show. Maybe have a set up next to hers? Beman, people will know you and greet you along the way, correct?" Conrad nodded. "Rina, you can do the old friend routine or introduce yourself. Whatever works." Rina nodded at Weston then shook her head to clear it out.

"My life is getting stranger by the minute."

"Pull this off Tangy, and you can see Doc in the morning…"

"What happened before the show?"

"No time."

"But, I am flying home after tonight…"

"About that… We changed it for you."

"You can't. I have a life, you know. I mean, what about work?"

"You are working on something down here."

"WHAT?"

"Trust me, Rina. This will all work out."

"I have no choice?" Weston nodded no as Rina reached back to rub the back of her neck. Weston and Wayback stood by the door, going over plans in the folder while Rina's mind wandered elsewhere. One hand rubbed the back of her neck, and the other rested on her cramping stomach. She breathed deep and closed her eyes.

At the concert hall, Weston flashed his ID, people smiled and let them pass. Rina just stared into the distance.

"You could at least be cordial," Weston stage whispered.

"Why? I am in a place that I don't want to be, surrounded by people I don't want to hang with. I'd rather be home cleaning my bathroom."

"You clean?"

Rina lifted her middle finger in the air.

"Nice…"

"Look, all I want to do is go home. How would you feel if someone wouldn't let you do what you wanted?"

"That never happens."

"Seriously? Does your ego ever take a day off?"

Weston laughed, "You are too much, Tangy."

He continued to show ID as they walked through the tunnel. With each pause, Rina would stand on her toes and touch her heels in the air. He could almost hear her muttering; there is no place like home. He walked Rina as far as the opening, then watched as she wandered over to the taping area. There was no hug or kiss good-bye today.

Rina placed her case on the floor and looked around the arena. Happy people greeted each other with big hugs, and laughter flowed in all directions. She opened her case and took out the tape deck, wires, batteries, and blank cassettes. Rina caught a Doc-look-alike out of the corner of her eye. When she stood for a better view, it turned out the guy just had Doc's hair. The rest wasn't even close.

"Crap," she commented to the universe. With shaking hands, she wrapped the wires around the mic stand, connecting one end to what she hoped was a stable microphone. She raised the stand up into the smoky air and connected the lower end of the cord to her tape deck.

Over by the soundboard, Wayback and Meth Head Biker Dude hugged each other and laughed aloud. Each man made an exchange, and then both would burst into laughter. Rina's stomach cramped up with each outburst.

"Crap," she repeated to no one. "I am so screwed."

"No, you are not," she heard a voice from behind her. The stoner dudes were back. Their set up was almost complete. "As long as you snapped the mic in that thingy on top, you should be fine," he looked up at the ceiling.

Rina sighed. "Yeah, I did snap the mic in, thanks."

"No Doc or Cowboy to help tonight?"

"Just me," Rina's eyes teared up. "Just me..."

"At least I have something pretty to look at." The crowd roared, the lights dimmed, and Rina was relieved she didn't have time to respond.

She looked back and shook her head, stretched her arms up, and stood on her tip-toes. Rina bent over to start the tape as someone plopped down in the chair next to her. She looked up to see Wayback's smiling face at the same time she hit the record button. Someone nudged her on the other side. Her head spun around to find Meth Head Biker Dude giving her a toothless smile. She struggled to sit up as something pinched her arm.

The lights faded. The crowd disappeared, and her world went silent.

Rina has been to shows coherent for years, so when a big purple teddy bear held her hand, and they skipped together in a circle to Tower Of Power's "What Is Hip," she knew she just had to stay positive and ride out the buzz. The trip was destined to only get stranger.

Fluffy white droplets floated through the air and went poof in her hands with every touch of her fingers. The big, fuzzy, purple teddy bear spun around to lead Rina through the dewdrops around in a circle, skipping, stepping, bobbing, and weaving. He would stop on occasion to bend over and shake his rear end in the direction of the sound.

Rina held onto his hand tight. "I feel like Alice, and you are my White Rabbit," she tried to say out loud. "Did I just say that?" she giggled. "Maybe? Maybe not…" She grasped his paw tighter. "Please don't lose me," she squeaked.

"Oh my lovely," the teddy bear responded in a much deeper voice then Rina expected. "I can't lose you," his expressionless face next to hers, "You are my prize!" He pulled her in the opposite direction back toward the sound.

"Your prize? How am I a prize?" Rina rushed to keep up. Breathless, she tried to move with the beat. Stinging pain vibrated through her armpits. "Armpits aren't supposed to hurt," she pondered. Rina fell to the floor as her butt enlarged to fill the space created for her. The big purple teddy bear fought to free his paw. She stretched as far as she could to catch him as he wandered into the white poofs, finally disappearing.

"Stop! Come back!" she screamed. Something warm covered her body.

Spheres moved around her body as Rina attempted to push herself up. She couldn't maneuver her legs to lift her behind from the floor. They kept slipping to the side while her butt expanded and got sucked into the floor. The poofs floated over her body, blocking the light in the room.

Darkness.
Bright lights.
No lights.
Bright lights.
The blinking hurt her head. She grabbed onto both sides. "I don't want my brain to explode," she pleaded. "Stop! I want to get off…"

Her eyes closed as her head sank into her hands. She rolled her body into a ball on the hard surface. Her life just wasn't as fun without the big purple teddy bear.

"I want the fluffy bear back," she whined.

Something bright was showing behind her eyelids as her head pulsated. "If I don't open my eyes, nothing bad can happen," she whispered. "If I keep my eyes closed, this will all be ok..."

"Come on, Sunshine..." Rina didn't recognize the voice. "Let us see those beautiful baby blues." The brightness faded away from her eyelids. She blinked her eyes open and focused on the man before her.

"She's awake," he reported. There were excited voices all around. Rina tried to lift her hands to hold her tender head. Her hands didn't move, and she couldn't turn her body in any direction.

"Who are you?" she whispered to the stranger.

"I was about to ask you the same question," the man had such a gentle smile. Warmth filled Rina's heart. She tried again to move, yet her legs wouldn't lift, torso wouldn't twist, and her arms, well, her arms were just stuck where they are.

"Am I tied down?" Rina asked.

"For your own safety," he replied.

"Oh." Rina tried to catch parts of any conversation happening around her. Yet, they all just meshed together in annoying white noise. She moved her eyes in each direction, picking up on little things. The room wasn't very big or well lit. She lay on a makeshift hospital bed or one of those adjustable ones you can buy at a cheesy furniture store. The more she moved her eyes, the less her head ached, and the more she could take in of her surroundings.

As in a real hospital, this room lacked the blinking lights and beeping machines. The only person she could actually see she named Dr. Smiley. And Dr. Smiley looked like a stereotypical TV doctor. He wore his dull brown hair short with a perfect cut. His eyes were kind and brown. He shaved, and his complexion was clear.

Rina took mental notes of every detail, although nothing about this guy stood out. He had an excellent upper body — defined arms with a possible six-pack. The lab coast wasn't that tight, yet it wasn't that loose either. Then it hit her - this guy was Dr. McDreamy on that show she never watched.

"So who are you?" she asked again.

"You first," he replied with a sexy smile.

"I don't like this game; I always lose at it. But ok… Rina."

"Where are you from?" he asked.

"Nope, my turn," she watched him cringe. "I've played this game before. Who are you?"

Dr. Smiley looked behind her before answering, "Dr. Winebox."

"Winebox, huh?" She added, "Where am I?"

He wiggled his long finger. "Nope. It is my turn. Where are you from?"

"Connecticut," then without thinking, Rina added, "What about you?"

"New York." Rina detected a zero New York accent. Her head beat again. "So…" she started to say.

"No, my turn." This time his voice became hard. "Where is Jacko?"

"Jacko, who?"

"Don't even go there," he scolded. "The guy you were traveling with before you got to DC. Yay tall, brown hair… Where is he?"

"You mean the Asshole?" Dr. Not-so-Smiley nodded as Rina's mind clouded. "He got arrested with my friend Doc. What an asshole that guy is…"

Someone muttered "Shit!" in the background as Rina found herself back with the big purple teddy bear. He held out his big purple paw. Rina stood, then they danced away down a golden green path through a meadow of bright blue daisies.

No music played. The bright fuscia sky held a sparkling orange sun. The sky and meadow extended toward an endless horizon. Rina and the teddy bear moved toward the horizon line as the colors around her became grays. The big purple teddy bear stopped to catch its breath.

Rina looked up in time to see Wayback kissing Luna in the distance. She started to stumble in their direction as the bear yanked her arm in the opposite.

"Ouch!" she screamed and pulled harder. The Luna figure looked into Rina's eyes and then disappeared into the mist.

"Crap…"

"What do you mean you lost her?" Weston barked at Beman. "All you had to do was keep an eye on her! How the…" He stomped over to stare at the pictures of the suspects taped to the wall: Jacko Manilla, Bruce Norton, Marshall Butmon, Neil Moon, and Tangerina Hanley.

"Boss listen to me," Beman pleaded. "I was sitting next to her in the taper's section. Next thing I know, it's half time, security is waking me up in my chair, and Rina is gone. I have no memory of what happened. The tape decks were turned on. Everything looked normal except…"

Weston cocked his fist back as Mary entered the room. "You don't want to do that boss," she said calmly. "Imagine the paperwork." Mary rested against the doorframe. It wasn't often she saw her boss losing it like this. She turned away so her boss couldn't see her smile.

Weston ran his fingers through his hair, then held his head tight. "Please tell me you got the tapes," he said through clenched teeth. Mary stood in silence. "Mary?"

"Something malfunctioned with our set up," she started to explain. "The monitors are currently down."

"Does that mean we can't watch the tapes, or there are no tapes?"

"At this point, I'm not sure," Mary shrugged. "I got the techs working on it and am trying to put together an eyewitness report. So far, we got Beman here sitting with Rina and 'some big dude' sitting on the other side…"

"Some big dude?"

"I asked the gentlemen sitting behind Rina, and his use of proper English was limited." Weston nodded. "Sometime during the first set 'the big dude' and Rina left, and according to the witness, she was smiling and happy and 'ready to party.'"

"Well, that is definitely not Rina because she never is happy." The room erupted with nervous laughter. "Okay, so we have her leaving, and Beman here waking up. What else?"

"That's just it, boss," Beman started. "I asked around, and no one saw her leave the building. At least no one could remember…"

"Can we bring in the guys behind her?"

"On what charges? Marijuana? We would have to arrest most of the audience."

"I don't know. Something. Can't we just interrogate them?"

Weston looked around the room at his crew. Most of them had been with him throughout the investigation while others, like Beman, transferred in from other areas. Beman was at one point working on the same case over at the DEA's office.

"Okay," Weston started to pace in the small space. "We need to search the entire building."

"Already in progress, boss," Weston cringed when Beman addressed him that way. "We've gone through the upper and middle tiers, and I have a couple of DC cops combing the tunnels."

"Good job. Please let me know if anything comes up," Weston said, although he already suspected nothing would be found. His gut told him he would need to cut ranks and make his circle even smaller. "Let's keep going in that direction for now, and Mary," she turned from the blank screens, "please let me know when we are back on line."

As the group turned to leave, Weston heard the comment, "At least someone gets a please." Weston followed through the tunnel and headed out to his car. He opened the driver's side door to reach under the seat and pull out a portable satellite phone. Placing the earpiece in, he dialed the unlisted number, committed to memory. The call was answered before the second ring.

"How did it go?" the familiar voice inquired.

"Good. Were you able to get the footage off the monitors and re-set up before the sabotage?"

"We got most of it. Weston, you are not going to like what is on these tapes."

"Beman is helping?"

"You got it."

"I had a feeling…"

"And that is why I put you on this one. Wes, you are the best at picking up nuances that others ignore. Do you think we are on the right track?

"I do, yet I should be able to confirm a couple things once I am contacted by the kidnappers."

"Weston, I know this one is hard for you. Please believe that Rina will be safe."

"Can you guarantee that, because I can't?"

"No, I can't. However, I do have my best agent breaking apart a major US drug distributorship, and I know he will make sure his gal is safe."

"She's not…"

"Weston, stop. I have seen your screensaver for God's sake. Look, you need to keep the focus on our main goal. Once all this is settled, and it will be, then you can swoon the gal." Weston laughed. "Weston, remember the hero always gets the gal."

"Thanks, Marty, but let's get the scum first." Weston hung up the phone and placed it back below his seat. He took his laptop out of the briefcase and began making notes from the evening. With his list complete, he began to review. The operation looked status quo until his last two notes: Mary had trouble finding the video; no one on his team saw Rina leave her seat.

He stared at both, trying to make sense of it all. A slight cramp in his stomach told him all he needed to know. He deleted the last two notes off his computer then sent the document over to Mary to add to the case file. Weston took out his pocket notepad and jotted down a few more notes before he wandered back to the makeshift camp.

The room appeared empty, with half the monitors producing static. In contrast, the others held shaky pictures from various angles of the concert hall. Unidentifiable gray figures roamed across the screens, pushing brooms or moving garbage cans. At times, two workers would stop, and random conversations would take place.

There appeared nothing out of the ordinary.

Half of his crew followed up on imaginary leads while the other half, the ones he had concerns about, probably met at an all-night diner or someone's house. It was his job to uncover which people played for which team.

"Mr. Traynor?" Weston turned to see a DC police sergeant standing in the doorway.

"Yes." He reached over to shake the officer's hand.

"My boys have swept the venue and the surrounding area..." Weston observed the man rocking on his heels, "unfortunately, no one has turned up at this time. Would you like us to increase our area?"

Weston shook his head no. "The agency appreciates all you have done for us," Weston replied. "I've got some of my guys pursuing leads." The sergeant turned to leave and then stopped.

"If I may, there is one thing that is bothering me, though." Weston waited for the man to continue, "No one just disappears. There is always a trail somewhere. My boys were everywhere tonight. So how did she leave?"

"That, my friend, is the million-dollar question." Weston grabbed his briefcase and moved at a slow pace toward his car. The road crew moved crates up on to a tractor-trailer. The band's bus was long gone taking with it their followers.

"Yes, we checked the trucks, band bus, and everywhere in between…" Weston turned to see Mary standing behind him.

"I didn't know you were still here…"

"I was just getting the reports and the videos together. I figured you would want them on your desk in a few hours."

Weston indicated agreement, "You got that right." Both moved toward the unmarked cars. Only three vehicles remained. Weston took note of the third car yet said nothing. "Thank you for your help, Mary. Go get some sleep. We can start looking at the evidence in the morning."

"You are pretty calm boss. Do you know something I don't?" She raised her eyebrow and gave a toothless smile.

"Actually, you probably know more than me," he gaffed. "Can I tell you something, Mary, just between us?" Mary leaned in, "My focus is on getting Rina back. I can't believe I went with this hair-brained scheme. My ego thought I could keep her safe, but now…" Weston turned away as Mary swept him into a motherly hug.

"It will be okay, boss. We will get her back."

Weston shook his head, hiding his face from her view. "Good night Mary," he choked as he opened the car door and got into the driver's seat.

Once on the road, he smiled. The set up complete, now he needed to wait.

Instead of stopping on his floor, he continued up to the guest bedroom. The comforter still had the outline of where Rina had slept. He lay down in her space and breathed in deep. The smell of fresh flowers, patchouli, and rain-filled his nose. "Oh, Rina. I hope I haven't done something stupid again..." he muttered as he drifted off to sleep.

"I got her here, you idiot!" A deep voice boomed in the distance. "Don't you believe me?" A clicking noise, along with a bright flash, entered Rina's consciousness. She opened one eye then closed it again.

Rina then opened both eyes and cringed. Her left arm felt fuzzy. Her wrist was attached to a fluffy handcuff attached to the end of a brass bed. She sat on a bright, white, old-fashioned bedspread, the type with bumps in the fabric for the pattern. She touched the material with her other hand while her thoughts wandered to her grandma's guest room.

Her grandma's guest room had crystal doorknobs she used to think were big diamonds, high ceilings, and big windows that overlooked a busy street. When she slept over, her grandpa would sing "Goodnight Irene," while she'd drift off into a night of safe sleep. A warm feeling surrounded her and then just as quickly left.

The bedspread appeared to be the only similarity. The walls had been colored in Pepto-

Bismol pink with bright white lace curtains swaying in the window. Each movement of the curtains brought another blast of warm, humid air into the room. A large chest took up the entire side of the wall across from the single door.

Attached to the bed, Rina was wholly clothed, with a slight headache that leaned more toward hangover than the flu. She didn't feel right, yet she was alive. At least for now.

"What do you mean why? I did what you said!" The loud voice from the other side of the door caught her attention. She giggled as she wondered who they were talking about.

"I sent Weston the picture..." Rina leaned closer. "Of course he freaked out. That was half the fun." Her breaths started to come faster. "Well yeah. The girl is really cute..." Rina inhaled and held the air deep inside her swirling stomach. "I know. I know—no touchy. I wouldn't anyways. I think she'd bite my balls off..." Another voice joined the laughter. "Yeah, she looks demented. So what's the plan?"

Rina stretched out on the bed, measuring how far around the room, her body could move. She pulled on the handcuffs, making more noise than progress with getting free. Her stomach growled, a gentle reminder that she hadn't eaten in a while.

Outside the window, silence. The breeze provided nothing—no smell or bird sound. Rina sat back on the bed. Through her jumbled thoughts, the question of why she was here kept coming back.

"Weston, what have you gotten me into now?" she murmured. The door opened, and a tall, thin man entered. Without a word, he put a fast-food bag next to her. "I don't eat burger crap," commented Rina, wrinkled her nose for effect, then adding, "And I want to know why I am here, like this." She held up her attached wrist to emphasize her point.

The tall man put on a thin smile. "That is your dinner," he pointed. His voice came out too deep for his body. It didn't match the overly skinny twenty-something standing in front of her.

"I don't eat meat or fast food," Rina replied. If she could have crossed her arms, she would have.

"Then, you go hungry. Ba, ba, ba." Tall and skinny laughed. Rina studied the features of the person in front of her. His bird-like face held nothing special—no scars or beauty marks or tattoos. The man would just blend in where ever he went. He dressed in worn jeans and a pocket t-shirt with no brand sneakers.

Rina saw guys like this every day at the casino. They wanted to stand out and be special yet blended into a crowd so nice. In this case, he knew he had the upper hand and would probably take advantage of that. The casino crawled with people who knew the angles too. Rina and her boss referred to them as the slime suckers. Jacko, the Asshole was one also.

"I suppose you don't drink soda, either?" He asked. Rina shook her head no. "I can't let you starve. What would you eat?"

"Power Veggie Bars," Rina blurted. "You can get them at Health Foods." Rina held her breath, waiting for an answer. If he said okay, then she was close to a city or a suburb. The oh-so-trendy grocer Health Foods would not open a store in a rural area.

"Try again," the man sighed, his patience waning. "How about a hippie grilled cheese?" he asked hopefully.

"How about a straight one?" He nodded, turned, and shut the door behind him. He returned with white bread soaked in grease with American orange cheese seeping out at the crusts.

Rina wrinkled her nose then was quick to add, "thank you." She ate around the edges until the amount of fat started to turn her stomach. A phone rang in the distance. The first voice barked, "Hello."

"Yeah." By the anger in shrill stranger's voice, Rina decided that Grilled Cheese Dude was neither a chef nor in charge of her current situation. She took the rest of the bread and rubbed her handcuffed wrist as she pulled the metal out toward her fingers. The butter dripped on the spread, and the cuffs left a red ring around her wrist, but would not slip over her thumb and palm. "Crap," she muttered at the same time the door opened.

"Don't believe me," the shrill voice screamed. "Take this to the princess." Grilled Cheese Man entered holding onto a cellphone. He spotted Rina's wrist and shook his head as he placed the phone near her mouth.

"I'm going to have to clean that," he pointed at the butter stain. "Say hello," he instructed while he tapped his foot.

"Hello," Rina panted into the speaker.

"Tangy, is that you?" Weston's voice came through.

"Don't call me that," she replied before adding, "What the heck, Wes?" A shadow moved around the next room. Grilled Cheese Man turned to walk away with the phone. "I don't think we were done talking," Rina shouted.

"Yeah, you were," Grilled Cheese Man said.

"See Tangy," a shrill voice said with contempt, "is alive and well, Weston. For now, at least…" Shrill voice must have turned off the speaker because Rina couldn't hear Weston's reply. "Hell, she just had a gourmet meal," he laughed. "Look, you want the princess back or what?"

"He better be saying yes, or I'll kill him myself," Rina muttered in the silence. She heard a laugh from the door where Grilled Cheese Man still lurked in the shadows.

"Yeah, I thought you would feel that way. It's pretty simple, Wes," the shrill voice said. "You have something I need, and I have something of yours…" The silence in between had Rina stretching to hear. "You idiot, I need Jacko." Rina tried to get closer to the door. "Look, man, your gal here is pretty cute. I would hate…"

The conversation continued while Rina assessed her current situation: handcuffed to a bed, eating lousy food, whereabouts unknown. That about summed it up.

"I am so screwed," Rina shook her head and started rambling. "I knew Jacko was an asshole. I knew that Doc should have left him in New York, especially after that party. Better yet, we never should have let him in the car with us. I mean, really, how dumb can Doc be? And the worst part of all this," she took in a deep breath, "I told Doc that but…" She sat and shook her head, getting angrier with each movement. "Doc's an idiot too. Crap, all the men I surround myself with are imbeciles. Look at me," she held her wrists up to no one, "I mean really, who does this?" Rina took in a deep breath. She didn't notice Grilled Cheese Man had moved back into view of the doorway with a glass of clear liquid. She looked up and started to repeat, "I am so screwed," to which he just nodded in return.

Weston hung up the phone, leaned over his desk, and said nothing, while Conrad Beman, Mary, and the rest of his team sat around the glass table in silence. "Anyone here recognizes that voice?" he finally asked. Looking over his side, one by one, each gave a head nod no. "Okay, Mary, when will we have the trace on the number ready?"

"Give my team three more minutes, Wes, and we should at least have a radius."

"Good." Weston looked into Mary's eyes. She didn't flinch and, in his mind, had an air of defiance. "Good. Thank you. Interrupt with the info at any time." Weston looked around the room again and waited for input from his team. "The rest of you think about the voice. We will have a replay in five in the conference room. From that and the radius, we should be able to track this."

"Boss, you think this is where Jacko's people are?" Conrad questioned.

"Not sure. My gut tells me that someone associated with him must be responsible for this. I'm not sure how high up the food chain we are at this point…" He hesitated. "Let's get to the conference room. I will be there in three." Conrad and the three other members got up and left the office. Mary stood by his desk.

"You okay, boss?"

"Sure, Mary. Why?" Weston replied with a bit more hostility than he should have. Catching himself, he added, "Just frustrated. I'm regretting making her part of this. She didn't deserve this."

"No, she doesn't, but she is involved now," Mary replied. "I got a radius down by a beach just south of here in Virginia. Should we send a team?"

"No."

"No?" Mary stood straight up. "Really, boss? You are just going to leave her there?"

"For now, Mary." Weston stood to signal the end of their conversation. "And please, shut the door when you leave." He watched Mary exit then waited for a beat before taking out his other phone.

"What have you got, Marty?"

"She wasn't lying. There is an abandoned beach area in Easton, Virginia that the signal came from. This is a rundown beach community that residents left after the last storm, and from what I can see, they haven't been back in years. There are lots of homeless and delinquents in the area. What are you thinking?"

Weston sighed. "I'm thinking that this is just a diversion. I also think that our friend Wayback—"

"You mean our agent Beman?"

"Yes, that is exactly what I mean. He and his crew are toying with us, buying time by using Rina. And I think there is still a missing piece we haven't figured out yet. There is something that Jacko had on him that we can't find. Why else would a small-time dealer gather this much attention?"

"You know I had the same thought. I have my team looking into shipments coming in via water. You and I are both on the same path here, buddy. What do you think he has?"

"I'm not sure, yet Rina said something about a list. You don't think he would be dumb enough to carry a distribution list with him, do you?"

"You never know Wes. Some people think they are invincible, above the law."

"That is true. I feel like I am surrounded by some of them. They actually keep us in business," Weston let out a forced laugh. "So, what is our next move? I don't think I should send my team in. I have trust issues happening here."

"You could be on target there. We are watching Mary and Conrad as requested. There is also a third agent, Wilson, who has been in a strange company lately."

"Wilson missed my briefing this morning. He said something about kids in a play. I don't know. I didn't even know he had kids."

"Not sure he does. Anyway, he is on our radar too." Weston looked over his note pad. "Wes, you need to move really careful from here on out. This whole thing is going to get stranger. I can feel it."

"Yeah, I feel it too, Marty. Me too." Weston looked back at his notes, circling the radius for the beach house. "I will keep you posted. I have a feeling I am going to be hearing from those idiots again soon."

"I hope Rina stays safe, Weston."

"She's tough, boss. Let's just hope she doesn't kill me when all this is over." Weston heard laughter then hung up the phone. He placed it back in his briefcase, along with his personal notepad. He glanced up at his screen saver to the photo of Rina. She smiled back. He touched the side of the screen and sent the view back to file folders. Weston grabbed his briefcase, walked over to his office door, and opened it. Mary stood by the filing cabinet closest to the door. She flinched, then turned and smiled.

"Everyone is in the conference room, boss," she directed.

"Thanks, Mary. I am not sure what I would do without you," Weston smiled back. She followed Weston through the carpeted maze. Voices grew louder as they approached the glass door. Through the door, Mary and Weston watched their other colleagues in a heated discussion. Weston smirked but changed his expression to concern as they opened the door. Silence fell over the room as people sat in frustration, exchanging concerned glances. No one would look direct at Weston, but Weston looked at each team member. The only one who appeared pleased was Mary, who sat over in the corner. With the reflections in the glass, this position befitted her option to observe all present.

"What is going on, boys?" Weston asked.

"We got a call, boss," someone blurted out.

"From the kidnappers..." another voice expanded.

"And I wasn't notified, why?" Weston asked through gritted teeth. He placed both hands on the table as he stared down his team.

"That would be my fault," Conrad confessed. "I called Mary, and she said you were on the phone with someone higher up..." he waited for Weston to confirm. When he just got an icy stare in return, Conrad continued, "So I took the call."

"We ran a trace, and the signal came from the same area as before," Mary chimed in.

Weston nodded and jotted down a few notes. "And?"

"They said they would like to make a trade."

"A trade?" Weston looked confused. "What on earth do they want to trade for? They would be insane to think that Rina is worth Jacko." The room became uncomfortably silent. Weston looked at each of his team members and then shook his head. "You have got to be kidding me. You didn't…"

"No, I didn't," Conrad replied. "I said that it was up to you." He sat back and crossed his skinny arms over his chest. With Conrad's arms in the crossed position, Weston noticed a small spider tattoo on Conrad's wrist, similar to one specified in Jacko's file.

"What was up to me? I need details." He turned towards Mary, "When will the tape be ready?"

"There is no tape," Mary replied.

"And why is there no tape? This is the FBI. We record everything."

"Because they called on the secure line…"

"The secured line?" Weston hesitated.

"Yeah, the secured line. Here are my notes." Conrad slid his notepad across the table. Weston looked at the first sentence: *The princess for Jacko.*

"Rina for Jacko. Is this guy serious?"

"Keep reading, boss," Conrad instructed.

Weston looked down at the other notes, cringing with each demand. *Weston brings Jacko. He can have a driver, but no one else. Any sign of an ambush and the first bullet goes in Rina's heart.*

"These people think that Rina is more important to me than she is." He looked around the room. "There is no time or place on here," he noted.

"They said they would get back to us…"

"Great. Let me know when they do."

"You want me to drive, boss?" Conrad asked.

"No. I think you need to go back undercover as Wayback. I'll get one of the guys from the pool to drive me." Weston hesitated. "When you catch up with your tour buddies, do some digging into where these Jacko's contacts have property, even if they are casual contacts like Doc."

"We already did that boss. These people… they are like air. They are everywhere and nowhere if you know what I mean. Kind of like drifters."

"Conrad, please do not get dramatic on me." Weston abruptly turned toward the door, "I have to see what is going on with our prisoners, then get this Rina thing taken care of." *This Rina thing?* Weston watched Mary's reflection mouth to Conrad.

"You going to spring, Jacko, boss?"

"Maybe." Weston slammed his hands down on the table. "Yes. As crazy as it sounds, I am going to try to release Jacko." He watched Mary's eyes twinkle then added, "Get me a time and place."

"Should I arrange a car and driver?" Mary asked.

"Please do," Weston replied. "Thank you, Mary. I am heading over to see about Jacko. Let me know when you have something new."

Weston headed toward the holding area, then, once out of view, took the elevator to the sixth floor. He walked with purpose toward the end of the hall, knocked twice, and entered the room, where Marty sat in the dark, watching a monitor. The group had continued talking after Weston's exit.

"Please arrest whoever Mary sends as my driver," Weston said as he took the seat next to his old boss. "This all really sucks Marty."

"Yeah, big time," Marty responded. He turned toward Weston. "You are doing the right thing here. We can't have our department compromised."

"I know. It is just funny that two years ago, you sent us a new Porsche..."

"That and Vegas gambling debts," Marty laughed. "Look, Wes, the shit that Butman caused is not your fault."

"I'm the one who got suspicious."

"No, you are the one who vocalized your suspicions. I had a file, remember?"

"Speaking of Butman, Rina calls him Meth Head Biker Dude." The two laughed.

"I think that will be his new code name. How about you?" The two men turned their attention back to the screens. Mary stood in the corner, speaking on a portable phone. Only she and Conrad remained.

"Where did the others go?"

"Not sure how far in they are. The reason you walked in on an argument was that Conrad announced the kidnappers had made contact, and the rest was pissed that he hadn't called them back from the break room."

"You think Conrad's in charge?"

"No!" Marty laughed. "I think Conrad is Butman's eyes and ears here. Butman knows something has been up since we arrested Jacko without him."

"What about Mary?"

"Not sure about her. There may be something going on there, yet her loyalty is torn."

"What makes you say that?"

"She made a comment to Conrad about this getting out of hand. I think she is maybe feeling guilty."

"Or she knows she is being watched and is covering her tracks?" Marty nodded. Weston continued, "Mary is smart and has mentioned wanting to work in the field at various times."

"Have you allowed her in any cases?"

"Just this one and the work she is doing is mostly observational."

"Any complaints?" Weston nodded, no. "We should keep an eye on her too." Marty sighed. A bing sound escaped from Weston's briefcase. As he removed a second phone, Marty watched Mary on the monitor.

"Yeah," Weston answered. He listened carefully as he jotted down notes. "And who is my driver?" Weston wrote down the name then turned the pad towards Marty. Marty scribbled something below. Weston nodded. "Mary, let's have the driver meet me downstairs instead of in my office. Say at…" he watched Marty scribble a time. "Two, then we can go over the plan while we ride over. Yeah. Thanks." Weston listened. This time he observed Mary and Conrad on the monitor. "No, I'm not coming back to the office. I need to make a couple of stops first." Before Mary could continue, he added, "Thanks for taking care of all this," then hung up.

Marty turned up the monitor volume and hit record. "Are we all set?" Conrad asked. "He said he is good to go," Mary replied. "And you confirmed Agent Marconi as the driver?" Mary shook her head. "Good. Do you think he knows?" Mary hesitated then replied, "Not at this point, but I think if we don't take care of business now…" Conrad nodded.

Marty and Weston sat in silence as they watched the two leave the conference room. Weston turned in his chair. "So, my driver…"

"Unfortunately is not going to be Agent Marconi. We will pick him up before he gets to the garage. We will get Harper up here to go with you. He is a sharpshooter along with a sixth-degree black belt."

"My kind of guy."

"Actually, he is. You two would get along like brothers on the same team. Listen, Wes, you can't take Jacko…"

"I know. I have another strategy."

"Do I want to know?"

"Probably not, so I will keep you posted."

"Good luck, kid." Weston nodded and then left Marty to continue watching the monitors, caught up in the soap opera of his job.

"Come on, princess. We are moving." Grilled Cheese Man placed a gag across Rina's mouth, and then covered her eyes with a bandana. The handcuff was released from the bed and used to hold her hands behind her back.

The cloth in her mouth tasted like salt and Coca-Cola, and though her nose and brain kept telling her that she had a dirty dishtowel in her mouth, she concentrated on breathing.

Rina shuffled along, trying not to trip over the rocks, or slide in the sand, or bump into those around her. When she did, a muffled, "Excuse me," escaped her lips. Cowboy was in the hospital. Doc was in jail. Rina was, well, she wasn't exactly sure where she was or what was going on. Whatever her situation, being bound and gagged couldn't be good.

Wayback popped into her mind. Why hadn't he helped her like he was supposed to? Crap he was probably in the hospital too. When she thought back to the concert, all she could remember was starting the tape deck and then dancing with a big purple teddy bear.

A heavy hand pushed down on top of her head, forcing her to squat like a dog. A rush of cold air then an icy feeling on her backside told her she was in someone's car. She most likely sat in the back seat. A touch of warmth greeted her on both sides.

She was surrounded in silence.

Her body moved to the beat of the road. It was challenging to stay in her own space with her hands tied up. As she bounced against the people on either side, she tried to stay alert. Keeping alert would keep her alive, she convinced herself. Alive, she could try to escape this mess. Dead, there wasn't much she could do except haunt Weston for revenge.

A ringing phone broke the silence. As the car came to an abrupt stop, Rina banged forward into the front seat.

"Hang on," the door opened, sending in a rush of warm air. The car shifted, and someone's hot breath was running down her right arm. The door opened again, and the car sunk to the right. A twist of acidity entered Rina's stomach. The only sound was the ripping of paper.

"Just follow the damn directions," sneered the shrill voice in charge.

Rina went back to the bounce and swirl. She attempted to get a song in her head to occupy her mind. She started to move to an unknown beat, rocking just her head and shoulders.

Then she started to hum "Amazing Grace," and before she could stop herself, the muffled words flowed from under her gag. In Rina's mind, she was belting it out like Joni Mitchell at Woodstock. In reality, she was bouncing between two big bodies and moaning like an animal.

The car stopped. This time an arm came across to keep her from slamming into the front seat. On the way back, a hand brushed against her breasts.

Slap!

"What?"

"Shush."

Rina shook her head, at No Touchy and Slap-stick. What a couple of buffoons!

##

A warm breeze rushed in as Rina's body slid across the cold seat. A hand positioned on top of her head tilted it to the side. Two hands-on each elbow assisted her into a standing position. The sun shone brightly through the bandana while its rays burned against her bare skin. Again, she stumbled and sunk, as she moved across what felt like sand.

No one spoke. On each side, a person held an arm. Another goon walked behind and kept stepping on the back of her shoe.

"I told you on the phone that she doesn't know anything," called out a gruff, authoritative voice that sounded a lot like Weston.

"No, shit. Did you bring my buddy?" Called out No Touchy

"Wouldn't be a fair trade, would it?" Though Rina heard whispering all around her, the only word she could make out was "shit."

"Come on, you know she was just in the wrong place at the wrong time."

"Happens to all of us…"

"So I can have her," said No Touchy, the buffoon who tried to feel her up in the car. He lightly traced a finger across Rina's cheek. He moved slowly down her throat and rested his hand between her breasts. She tried to shake him away, but the two escorts held on tighter. While laughter filled the air, puke filled her mouth.

"I would prefer you would leave the lady alone," Weston said. "We need her back, untouched." The hand moved away.

"We had an agreement, no?" A new voice arrived at the party. Rina shook her head and let spit into the gag.

"Look, if I gave you Jacko now, you would kill him, right?" When no one responded, Weston continued. "I need Jacko for a few more days. Then he's all yours, but I need to get your hostage back, untouched."

More silence.

"She hasn't been touched, right," Weston's voice continued. "Hey Tangy, besides that rude gesture, just now has anyone laid a hand on you?"

Something hard poked in the center of her back. After she nodded, no, it went away.

"I don't want her." No Touchy insisted.

"Well, neither do I, really. She is kind of a pain in the ass."

Rina heard laughs along with a couple, "You got that right."

"I'll tell you what—you give me the princess and take one of my guys or me."

"Take a federal agent? Are you serious? No. We keep the girl, and we try this again in exactly forty-eight hours. I will call the place." After more shuffling, Rina felt a hand on her head, she squatted down and was put back in the car. Her stomach turned as rage rose and fell in the back of her throat. She wanted to scream. Instead of singing "Amazing Grace" on the way back, she plotted her revenge on Weston. Being around Wes, she kept getting distracted by that same old rush he used to give her. That ship had sailed today.

"Hero, my ass," she mumbled.

          "Please tell me you got the tracker on the car," Weston said as he slid into the passenger's seat.

          "I couldn't get near it, so I tried a suction job. It stuck to the right side and hopefully melted against the metal before they noticed." Harper waited for a beat before adding, "Did you really expect those idiots to take one of us?"

          "No, but I had to try to say something to stall them. I didn't expect a second car, either."

          "That was a good thing," Harper added from the driver's seat. "It gave us a little more ground cover." The car pulled over in a secluded area under a canopy of oak trees. "You did notice she got pissed, right?" When Weston didn't answer, Harper continued to say, "You ever think that maybe you should have let her get busted too?"

          "All the time, but it is too late for that now. Is the tracker working?"

"Yes. They are heading south back toward the beach." Harper waited for a beat then asked,

"Should we follow?"

"No," Weston hesitated. "We just need their local for right now. Let's head back to the rendezvous point and see what the others found."

Harper turned the car back toward the office—a nondescript and abandoned office building Marty used to set up operations outside of the department. The windows were blackened, and the parking garage boarded up to avoid curiosity.

Though the investigation started out as a co-operation between the two departments, Weston was now the only person outside of Marty's team left on the taskforce. Unfortunately, as more information surfaced, so did more questions about some of Weston's team. The working theory posed that Marshall Butman, a bad apple from the DEA, managed to recruit several others from the FBI to set him up to take the fall if they were caught. Marty wasn't sure whether Weston had been targeted or if he was just in the wrong place at the wrong time. He really didn't care either.

It was fortunate for Weston that besides being related, he and Marty went back to basic training and had done a few co-missions overseas. At one point, they even dated sisters.

Marty was like the brother Weston never had. That was Butman's first mistake.

Hooking Jacko up with someone associated with Rina was his second.

The dim-lit hallway led to a conference room with top to bottom monitors on two walls. Stationed throughout, retired Marines, now part of Marty's team, and scanned the screens with blank eyes. One looked into Weston's department. Another trailed a bouncing dot toward the shoreline. A third set watched a warehouse, heavily guarded, down by the old military center.

Marty walked in carrying a half turkey on wheat in one hand and a file folder in the other. "Here is what we got so far. A shipment of heroin is arriving tomorrow night via boat. Butman and crew are to help escort the merchandise off the property. Jacko supposedly has the list of where everything is supposed to go. Wes, I have to ask, did you search her backpack again?"

"I did Marty, and there is nothing there. He must have hidden it someplace else."

"Butman and crew think your gal has it. That list has names, dates, places, and just about all the evidence we need to round up everyone. Weston, you know Jacko is small potatoes, and getting Butman will be easy now that we added kidnapping to his sins…" Marty took a bite of his sandwich.

"We need the list," Weston finished his thoughts.

"Yeah, that would be good." Marty started to walk out, then stopped to add, "Maybe it's in the taping stuff? You know the other kid's backpack?"

"I'll check again. It would be great if I knew what I was looking for."

"Yeah, it's the missing piece of a puzzle we can't even picture."

Rina's new room was different. The sky blue walls were wrapped in sailboat wallpaper. Rina could hear seagulls screeching out the lone window along with the rhythmic sounds of water breaking on the rocks. The smell was different too. Beach houses like this always had a musty, salty type of scent. That and the defunct fish smell of low tide.

The house must have been abandoned for a while. With no bed to chain her, the captors were forced to let her wander. Her new space had a futon on the floor and a couple of toss pillows. The futon took up almost the entire area anyway, leaving just enough room for the locked door on the opposite side to open. The single window was boarded up with new screws and plywood, but a window is still a window, Rina thought.

"Why is she still here?" A booming voice on the other side of her door sent cold goosebumps up Rina's arm.

"He wouldn't take her," No Touchy babbled. "He said she didn't matter."

"He's got her picture on his screensaver! He's bluffing!" the voice stormed. "You people are idiots!" After some back and forth shouting, something smacked against the wall.

"Can I have her to play with?"

There came another smack.

"No, you can't. She goes back in one piece…" The footsteps grew louder. "We need a plan."

"He said he needed Jacko for two more days, then he'd do the switch," No Touchy added.

"What kind of hostage-negotiator is he? I can't believe he's that stupid. Well, something must be happening in two-days. Look at the schedule!"

Rina heard papers rustle then, "Shit!"

Silence.

Rina moved back to the opposite wall and slid to a squatting position. She took a deep breath, held it for a ten count, and released it to ten counts. She looked back at the board on the window. It would take a few hours to get the screws out with a nail file, but she didn't have a nail file.

She could kick it out quickly if she had boots on, and the noise didn't matter. Looked like she would have to rely on Weston to save her. Rina laughed. In a tight whisper, she spoke to the ceiling, "Weston, I am going to kill you. And if these idiots kill me first, I will haunt you for the rest of your life. I will make sure you never get laid again. And I will do the same thing to Doc for letting that Asshole ride with us in the first place."

Though Rina had plenty more curses to plot, the door creaked open, and Meth Head Biker dude's body filled the space. "Hello, Tangy," he cooed. Rina brought herself to a standing position, crossed her arms, and attempted to return his stare down. "I hope you are enjoying your accommodations."

"Not really," she answered with a shrug. "What can I do?" Seemed lately, that was the question she asked all of the men in her life.

"Actually, you can leave very soon. I just have a few questions for you, and if you can help me out, well, we can probably make arrangements for you to leave. Immediately."

When Rina nodded, Meth Head Biker Dude continued, "Where did you go in New York City with Jacko?"

"We went to the big hotel on the south side of Central Park. I can't remember the name of it…"

"I don't care where you stayed. Where else did you go?"

"I didn't go anywhere else. Jacko and Doc took off for a while and drove someplace while I stayed in my hotel room. When they got back, I still stayed in my room. They had people with them, but it didn't sound fun..."

"Why not?"

"I don't know. It sounded like a bunch of drunks in the other room, and some chick with an accent kept yelling 'Arriba!' Plus, Doc had asked me to stay out of sight before they left, and once I heard the Arriba-chick, it was easy to do."

"Really?"

"Yeah, really. I have no reason to lie to you." Meth Head Biker Dude gave Rina the staredown, but she didn't budge. "You know the more you look at me like that, the more pissed off I get at the men in my life."

"Do tell," Meth Head smirked.

"First, Doc gives your asshole friend a ride, probably for the money, and we all end up in this huge mess." Rina threw her hands in the air. "So Doc gets thrown in jail. Then I send Cowboy out to help, and he ends up the hospital. I'm stuck here, well I am not exactly sure about *where* I am stuck. And don't get me started on Wes."

"Oh please, do start on Agent Traynor..."

"Well, Weston said he would protect me, then every time I need him, you show up instead. Back there, when he was supposed to save my ass, he just leaves me with you guys. 'Just need a couple of days, guys.' I should have known he would complicate my life. He did it before too. He wanted me to move to freakin', Alabama! By myself!" Rina screamed, "Who does that? I mean, people break up for a reason, right?"

"What the..."

"I mean, come on. Seriously, I shouldn't be here," she got up to pace around the room. "I should be at the casino, dealing with idiot gamblers who think they are going to beat the house. I mean, really, does the house ever lose? You ever look around and notice the elaborate buildings casinos are in?" Rina turned back toward Meth Head. "I mean, where do you think they get the money for that? And you should know this: I know nothing! Nothing! I mean, really, the only reason I am here and not in jail is that my ex got cold feet and decided to pull me out *before* the drug bust."

"What?" Meth Head rubbed his hands over his shaved head. He left them gripping the sides. "What did you just say?"

"I said the only reason I am here..."

"I heard you!" He screamed, "Because your ex has you on his screen saver."

"I don't know what that's supposed to mean. He had another girlfriend who just moved out. Amber Something. And Wes and I broke up in high school."

"His gal got pissed because you were on his screensaver," Meth Head said.

"Screensaver, huh?"

"Yeah. You and him in shorts and T's. You look like you were hiking."

"I know the photo. We were hiking at the beach." Rina stopped herself before she added that she had the same picture framed in her living room. Whenever she remembered to dust, she would stop and wondered why it was still there, but when she reached out to move it, she found that she couldn't.

As Meth Head Biker Dude got up to leave, Rina called out, "Wait, how long are you going to keep me?"

Her captor looked Rina up and down and smiled, "You'll be gone soon enough."

"The least you could do is give me a book or a TV or something," Rina shouted through the closed door. As she looked between the door and the window, the twirlers in her stomach went on overdrive. There had to be a way out.

##

Grilled Cheese Man brought another butter-soaked sandwich for dinner.

"Can I get a glass of water too?" Rina requested, adding, "Please."

Grilled Cheese smiled and shut the door. Rina took the sandwich from the plate and picked around the crust. Though she hadn't eaten a meal in two days, the orange cheese still turned her stomach.

The room darkened, but without a clock, she couldn't be sure of the time. Grilled Cheese Man came back with a plastic bottle of cloudy liquid.

"Drink up, princess," he instructed from the doorway, dividing his attention between Rina and the commotion in the living room.

"Get him!"

"Oh, man, did you see that?"

As the screams at the TV grew louder, Grilled Cheese leaned further out the door.

Rina looked at the contents of the bottle and cringed. With Grilled Cheese Man's head turned away, she was careful to pour the contents between the futon and the wall, making sure none leaked out on to the floor. Grilled Cheese looked back in time to see her taking the bottle away from her lips.

He smiled and closed the door. Rina lay down on the bed and placing the empty dishes just out of reach. She slowed her breath, and remained awake, closing her eyes, only when the door handle clicked back open.

"I think the princess is sleeping," Grilled Cheese announced. Laughter came from behind him. He shut the door, and Rina waited, but the click of the lock did not follow him. She sat up and listened. The men were still hooting and hollering at the television.

"That umpire couldn't see with glasses on!"

"What? No way was he out!"

Voices boomed. The show must have switched from wrestling to baseball. Soon the noise had stopped, and only the play-by-play announcer could be heard. Rina rose to the door. As slow and quiet as possible, she inched the door open just wide enough to peak out.

On the couch, two men, one twice the size as the other, were snoring. The table in front of them was covered with beer cans and cigarette butts and something shiny and metallic.

Soft, rhythmic, grunting noises came from another room. Windows on both ends stood wide open and screen-less so that bugs were welcomed in along with the sea breeze. Of course, Rina found the door right behind the men sleeping on the couch.

She took a deep breath in and opened the door just wide enough for her body to fit out, pulling it almost closed behind her. She moved quickly to the closest windows and dove right through.

She hit the porch with a thud.

Moving on adrenaline, Rina hopped over the railing straight into scratchy bushes. Her skin burned. Rina rose to move through the tick-grass, away from what the dilapidated house.

With no moon, there wasn't much to see. She followed the swish sound toward the water, hoping to find a beach, a boat, another house, anything! Blades of grass cut into her legs, while mosquitoes swarmed around her head. With each step, Rina's heart pounded. She stepped on something slick that moved under her foot and jumped into the air. Her first instinct to scream was muffled by the thought that they would find her.

She turned to see the house fade into the night and listened. No shouting. No guys were running after her. Nothing. The stuff in the plastic bottle must have been pretty potent for her captures to not even bother locking the door.

She needed help, but from whom? And how was she to contact them?

"Who can I call?" she started to mumble. "Weston is an asshole. Plus, he already lost me once and refused to take me back." She walked a little slower through the seagrass. "I have no idea how I am going to get home without any money. Besides, I'm probably fired now for not showing up to deal today."

The bugs feasted on Rina's legs and arms. She tried to rub them off instead of making slapping noises, but that wasn't working. What didn't sting started to itch. She looked around. The only sign of lights were those coming from where she had left. As she walked along the sand, holding on to herself, the sinking feeling of doom settled in.

Half paying attention to what she was doing, her toe connected with something hard on the ground.

"Shit!" escaped from her throat before she could stop it as excruciating pain shot up her legs. Rina grabbed her throbbing foot and fell to the ground, where another hard object hit her skull.

Her world went black.

"Where did they find her?" Weston stared at the lifeless body in the hospital bed. Tubes ran up to Rina's nose to help her breathe. IVs stuck out of each arm. Her legs and arms covered with bites and scratches. A bandage taped across the side of her head. Weston's eyes got teary then he refocused.

"She was on a beach just south of the locator. The place is mostly dilapidated houses, abandoned since the last hurricane along."

"Was there anyone with her?"

"No, and we checked the house. It was empty when we got there." Conrad Beman stood just behind his boss, his eyes on Rina.

"What about the guy who found her? Tell me about him."

"There wasn't much to tell. The locals call him Homeless Pete, and apparently, he lives down there. He is just another person who functionally decided life was too much. According to the local enforcement, he lives in one of the abandoned buildings and keeps an eye on the place for them." Weston turned and raised an eyebrow toward Conrad. "I kid you not. He flagged down the patrol and directed them to the spot. Based on their reaction, finding body parts in the woods is nothing new, although they were stumped as to what to do with a live one." Conrad smirked.

"At least this one is alive," Weston added. A jolt of guilt ripped through his heart as he watched the monitors beep. Rina was alive, though barely.

"She's more than alive," the doctor added from behind a desk in the corner. "She looks worse than she is because of the cuts and scrapes. Right now, we have her under sedation, at least for the time being."

"When will you bring her out?" Conrad asked.

"It will probably be an hour or two. We want to make sure she doesn't go into shock. Would you like to be present?" Weston nodded, and the doctor made a note on the chart. "Okay, well, until then, she needs rest. I am going to ask to have the room cleared."

"Should I stay on guard, boss?" Beman offered.

Weston did his best to look him in the eye and say, "Actually, Conrad, you should get some sleep. I'll have Mary set up the guard, and I will take over once Rina's awake."

Conrad saluted then left the room.

Weston looked over at the doctor. "I can take it from here, doc," he instructed. The doctor shook his head no.

"She needs monitoring. A hospital person or I must be present at all times. Come on, Traynor, you know the rules."

"Is there somewhere I can make a call?" The doctor pointed toward the glass on the opposite wall.

"Observation room should be empty, and it is soundproof. Would that work?"

Weston headed through the door and checked the room for any microphones or intercoms that might be turned on. He watched Rina and the doctor for a minute before determining the doctor was just a medical professional.

He took out his phone and dialed Marty first. "How is she?" Marty inquired.

"Alive," Weston answered. "The doctor said she'll be fine, at least physically."

"I'm glad to hear that, Wes. Did your guys manage to pick up anyone at the house?"

"Unfortunately, we did not. The report Conrad filed said the house was empty when they got there, although I have no proof it was. One of your guys came across a Jane Doe on the police wire, and when I went down to investigate, we hit the jackpot."

"It is a good thing you got there first."

"I agree. Now on to the bigger fish. Marty, can you pull the same guard routine as last time? You know, send me someone cleared and pick up whoever Mary gives us?"

"Wes, are you sure she is involved in all this?"

"Positive. The Jane Doe that your guy saw came across my desk an hour after I was notified, and the reports are coming in incomplete."

"How do you know that they are incomplete?"

"There are situations I have been privy to that didn't end up on my desk. The reports from the stadium all contradict each other and…"

"I shouldn't question, you are usually on target."

Weston moved closer to the glass. "How much time to you need to get me some help here?"

"Soon as we hang up, I'll get the guard to you and the team in the lobby, although I think it is crazy that these people would try anything at a military hospital."

"I think we have pushed the desperate button, and rational thinking has gone out the window."

"When can I pick up the rest?"

"Marty, give me twelve hours to accumulate a bit more evidence. I want to make sure that whatever we have sticks. By then, you can start with Mary and Conrad and all the low hanging fruit."

"What about Meth Head?" Marty laughed.

"I have a feeling he is tired of the incompetency of his team. He will probably attempt this one himself."

"Did you have the list?"

"No, but I have a theory where it is. I think Rina had it the entire time without knowing. When she wakes up, I am going to ask. I know that is the major piece to our puzzle."

"You'll find it." Silence. "Let me get my team into place, and you do your thing. Keep in touch."

Weston hung up then pushed the door leading to Rina's room ajar.

"About how long, doc?"

"Figure at least an hour or so. Are you coming back in?"

"In a minute."

Weston closed the door then dialed his assistant. "Talk about feeling out of the loop," she commented after hearing how they found Rina. "Weston, not one of your team members, has filed with me."

"That is a concern, Mary."

"Right now, all my intelligence is from the local police, and they said a homeless guy found a Jane Doe passed out on the beach. I take it that Jane was Rina?"

"Yes, but now she is here at Washington General. I need a guard for the room…"

"Isn't Conrad there?"

"I sent him back to the office, but I am getting ready for a meeting with Moon. I want to make sure no one gets in to see her."

"Moon's awake?"

"Yep, and he wants to talk only to 'Rina's friend.' I guess that would be me, go figure."

"I guess so," Mary muttered. "I need to get someone on Rina right away."

"Please. And Mary, for security's sake, let's keep this one quiet between you and me. I think we may have access to the evidence needed to finally wrap this one."

"Really?"

"Yes, really. As soon as Rina wakes up, we should have it all."

"That's… great. Hey, let me go and get the guard arranged."

"Thanks, Mary." Weston disconnected and smiled. He looked back at Rina, and a twinge of guilt surfaced. He shouldn't be using her in this condition. Yet, with all of Marty's guys around, this was probably the safest place she could be.

He trusted Marty. And if that list they needed was tucked into her backpack somewhere, all the better.

Weston walked back into the room and sat on the edge of the bed. He brushed her hair off of her face and then stroked her cheek. A warm glow started in the pit of his stomach then moved where his hand touched. He looked back at the wires and tubes attached to her body. Leaning in towards her ear, he whispered, "Tangy, I do love you, and I promise to make up for all the pain I have caused."

Rina's head was spinning. Did she just hear Weston say he loved her? Her heart pounded. So long ago she needed to hear those words and he wouldn't or couldn't tell her, and when he finally did, she was left to wonder if she was worthy or he just wanted the sex.

"Or I am back in the dream scene," she giggled. In the distance, something beeped, but for the most part, Rina lay content with a combination buzz and hangover headache. "I'm back in the dream I want to wake up from," she sang, or at least she thought she sang. Someone or something touched her hand, her arm, her neck. The warm glow didn't appear. Her heart stayed steady. She took in a deep breath.

##

Several doctors stood around Rina's bed, checking her pulse and trying to decipher her mumbles. The process went slower than expected, as they erred on the side of caution.

Weston watched from behind the glass. Mary sat in the back of the room, analyzing the data as it came in from the team. Her eyes went back and forth between Weston pacing along the observation deck and the entrance to Rina's room. Her right leg bounced. A quiet buzzing sound interrupted his pace.

"Yeah," he moved fast to answer the phone. Mary noted when Westin turned that the device was unfamiliar to her. She typed an email then reached for her purse. "I understand. Are we able to accomplish that now?" The question followed by silence, Mary clutched her purse tighter. The laptop remained on the table. "I agree," Weston turned to look Mary straight in the eye. "It is now or never." He disconnected and continued to stare in silence.

"Should that conversation be part of this report?" she asked casually.

"It already is," Weston replied.

"What?"

"Nothing. Mary, I need you to stay close to the communication center. Something is off."

"What do you mean, boss?" Mary's hand slipped inside her purse. Her fingers tightened around the cold metal.

"I'm not sure," Weston paced. "I just have this strange feeling…" He watched Mary's arm relax, and her hand reappears on her lap. "Mary, there are parts of this that make no sense."

"Isn't that your job, to make sense of it all?"

"Exactly. I just… forget it. Please keep close to the communication center and let me know when something new comes in and Mary, let me know if something is off, too."

"Will do boss."

Weston tucked the phone back into his briefcase, then re-entered Rina's room. "How is it going, doc?"

"So far, so good, Mr. Traynor. The patient is reacting nicely to the meds and has been drifting in and out. I think we can get her relatively conscious within the hour."

"What does 'relatively conscious' mean?"

"She was pretty beat up when she came in, probably from running through that swamp. We think the bump on the head was from tripping, not foul play, although we cannot prove it. Also, keep in mind that she has been out of it for a while. We put her on some pretty strong painkillers, so we are working on getting her back without any damage to her brain."

"What about the rest of her?"

"The bug bites and scratches will heal normally. That is all surface stuff. It was the bump to her head that was most significant. Of course, lying in that water didn't help. That area was originally shut down by the EPA because beachgoers were getting a mystery sickness."

Weston looked on in disbelief. "The good part is we did test her for increased levels of mercury and other toxic waste. She had some yet not as much as one would think for the environment she was in."

"Bottom line, doc?"

"I will have her conscious soon, and we can take it from there. In this case, we have to wait and see which, if I remember correctly, waiting and seeing is not one of your strong points." The doctor turned and went back to watching the monitors. A nurse entered and nodded at Weston as she changed an IV bag. As he watched Rina breathe, his heart throbbed.

Weston sat in the chair next to the bed. He leaned forward to take Rina's hand into his. He rubbed his thumb over her palm, and for the first time in years, Weston prayed. "Dear God, please let Tangy be okay. I do love her and will try to do right by her. My life is complicated, as you know, and I didn't want her to become part of that. Yet now I know… Everything happens for a reason, right? You just brought her back. Please don't take her away from me again."

Rina's thumb moved in loose circles over Weston's hand. He jumped. "Doc, her thumb just moved."

"That's good," the doctor replied, and he glanced down at their attached hands. "It is just a matter of time until she will join us. Keep doing whatever it is you are doing."

Weston leaned over and brushed his lips over Rina's cheek. He held her hand and sat and waited.

##

Sparkles floated in front of Rina's eyes. Her world was sanitized, but something smelled terrible. She got a whiff of garbage. Old trash was floating around her, and green slime was clinging to her body. Needles poked up out of the sand like seedlings wanting to grow. Her toes and fingers moved without pain while her legs and arms lay heavy.

A squawk in the distance sounded seagull-esque. Rina laughed at her new word. She thought about Grilled Cheese Man and the globs of the yellow butter oozing from her body. "Yuck," she muttered. Some of the gambler's faces who frequented her blackjack table flashed in front of her. Smelly Man with his dirty fingernails and gold chains parked in the chair to the left. To her right, Business Dude appeared, half in the bag, thinking he was God's gift to all women as he tried to throw a chip down Rina's blouse. They weren't the worst, though. Sleaze Man, with his entourage of wannabe gangsters, always made her life hell when he sat front and center. He was the nicest guy when winning, but when he lost, he was determined to make everyone in his path just as miserable as he was.

"I need a new job," she murmured. "Actually, I need a new life." She couldn't go back on tour. Even if they picked up this round of drug dealers, there would always others waiting in the wing. She would be labeled a narc and outcast. No, her touring days were over. It was time for a new hobby. Or time to revisit an old one?

Weston's face appeared with his goofy smile. Crap. The purple teddy bear waved good-bye while two little girls with perky bows and flowered dresses danced around her. Not my kids, she concluded. They are too ordinary. My kids would be tomboys, wearing comfy shorts and tye-dyed t-shirts. They would have their long hair tied back in a ponytail and run around kicking soccer balls and hacky sacks.

The pictures of the children morphed into what Rina had envisioned. She would be with the family sitting in the bleachers cheering on her girls at their softball game. Of course, they would play softball, Rina smiled. A warm jolt shot up her arm. She looked at the two rings on her left hand. A plain white gold wedding band and a sapphire set amongst a few diamonds. The hand that held it had a matching plain white gold band on it too. When Rina followed the arm up to his face, she gasped.

This can't be, she thought.

##

Meth Head Biker Dude stood outside the elevator door deep in conversation with the guard on duty. Dressed in a blue three-piece Armani suit with a white button-down shirt and FBI issued tie, he fit the scene perfectly. His short brown wig covered his scalp, and if one looked closely, they might notice the foundation that almost covered his scar. On his left lapel sat a government-issued ID. Based on his appearances alone, anyone walking by would not think twice about him.

"Are we good?" he whispered.

"Payment received," the guard acknowledged. "By the way, you should know that the other lady left in a huff earlier."

"What other lady?"

"The older one you were with earlier." Meth Head Biker Dude poked a gun with a silencer on end into the space between the guard's bulletproof vest and his pants.

"What lady?" He asked through clenched teeth.

"You know, I am not sure who she was. I just know she left with haste. She practically ran over one of my guys in the hall." The gun slipped further inside his vest. "You know, the lady who was in the room with Traynor, too." The guard stage whispered.

"Thank you for that information," the gun slipped back behind his jacket. The two men nodded, and Meth Head Biker Dude moved into the observation room. He watched his old boss hold onto the hand of the woman in the bed. "That screensaver does mean something to him," he muttered. When his new boss entered the hospital room, Meth Head Biker Dude smiled and turned up the speaker.

"How is our girl?" Conrad asked. He walked around to the foot of the bed for a better view. Weston's eyes narrowed and then relaxed. He thought Marty had said they picked up Beman.

"She is doing okay. We were lucky she was found when she was, otherwise..." Weston shrugged in his direction. He glanced back at the observation area in time to catch a shadow move across the window.

Rina felt a warm hand in hers, and whenever the other person spoke, the hand's thumb would gently stroke her palm. She sighed as the men continued talking.

"What is her status now?" Conrad pretended to look at the chart hanging at the end of the bed. The doctor walked over and removed the clipboard from Conrad's hand with a loud sigh.

"We are at the wait-and-see point," Weston interjected. "Doc says she should wake up sometime soon, but he couldn't say when. She drifts in and out, although mostly it has been out."

"How long have you been here, boss?"

"Since this morning, when she came in. I'll hang around until she is ready to leave. They are saying that will be in a couple days, but I doubt she'll be able to travel far." Rina squeezed the hand. Weston felt her touch but didn't show a reaction. "You know, the best news was that I didn't totally screw this up," he followed with nervous laughter. Rina's eyes fluttered open and closed.

Weston gave her hand a squeeze. He leaned over and kissed her cheek. As quiet as he could, he whispered, "Try to keep your eyes closed and relax. Most of all, trust me."

"I was supposed to have a meeting with Moon. He is awake too, but…" Weston held up Rina's hand. "I couldn't leave."

"Do you want me to take that meeting?"

"Thanks, Conrad, but I already told them I'd be over in a couple hours." Weston watched Conrad glance back toward the two-way glass. "You know I could go for a cup of coffee and a bathroom break," Weston disengaged his hand and stood. "Do you mind taking over for five?"

"Not at all, boss. Take your time." The door squeaked open then the only sound in the room was the beeping of the monitors. A second squeak of the door, along with a soft breeze, brought Rina to attention. She tried to open her eyes. Faintly, she made out the outlines of two figures standing at the end of her bed.

"What is the plan, boss?"

Boss? Thought Rina, *Wes is getting coffee.*

"Do we take care of her here?"

"Yeah, we have to at this point."

Rina's stomach rolled. She knew that voice but from where. Faces flashed in front of her until it stopped at one. "She looks so cute lying there. What do you think? OD?"

"No, too suspicious. Did you take care of the guard?"

"This one is on my payroll, but the next shift will be more difficult." Silence. Rina breathed in deep, trying to keep her body from shaking. "He also keeps the doc busy, so we need to hurry."

"Waiting is too risky," Rina half-opened her eyes to watch the figure pace. "Have we found the ledger yet?"

"No. I ripped apart the roadie case and the other backpack, but both were clean. Jacko swore he put it with her stuff for safekeeping. I went through it all, but I don't know where else to look."

"Did Jacko tell you that?"

"It was in the reports from questioning after the bust. I was pulled, remember?"

The silence was broken only by the breeze on the far side of the room. The door squeaked open, and a shift of weight on the side of Rina's bed jolted her. Again the warm hand attached to hers.

"Get your coffee, boss?"

"No – I changed my mind. I think I'll get some shuteye and come back. Do you mind taking the first shift?"

"Whatever …" Rina squeezed Weston's hand again then forced her eyes open. They fluttered a little then closed tight.

"Tangy," she heard Wes whisper. "Are you there?" Rina's lips grew into a loopy smile. "Hey there…"

"It is hey, now," she whispered back. Weston broke out laughing. "Take me home," she added.

"Sounds like an offer buddy," Conrad commented from nearby.

"Maybe later." Weston leaned over and kissed Rina on the forehead.

"Get me out of here," she cooed. Her eyes watered with the zing from his kiss. "Please," she begged.

"Don't worry, you are in good hands," Conrad called from across the room.

"You are just a little banged up," Weston started to say.

Rina stared into his eyes, silently pleading for him to understand. "I'm ok," she replied. "Just sleepy. I can sleep…" Rina yelped as she stretched her legs and arms. Pain rocked from fingertips to toes.

The doctor rounded Weston's side to peak over at Rina. He then stood quiet in the back, watching her and the monitors at the same time.

"You are not okay. Hey doc, can I get some meds?" Rina watched Conrad grin.

"NO!" she screamed while convulsing in the bed. The doctor rushed over and fiddled with the IV bag until Rina settled in a semi-loopy manner.

"Okay, okay, Rina. No meds. We will just sit here. Just you and me," Weston moved his arm around her shoulder. Rina's head tilted into his body. "Conrad, I guess you are off the hook with guard duty."

"Yes sir," he glared into Rina's eyes. Her skin pricked. Even half-stoned, she could feel the evil.

"Hey, I need you to go back underground. See what the word is out there. Someone has to have heard something."

"Yes sir," The door creaked open then stopped. "Sir?"

"Yes?"

"We are looking for a needle in a haystack or, in our case, a backpack among the following."

"What do you mean?"

"We have searched Bruce and Jacko's stuff..."

"And Rina and Cowboy's..."

"Then the bureau stripped the car, and that was clean."

"Where are you going with this?"

"Well, have we given any thought that Jacko knew we were on to him and ditched it before DC?"

"Or he gave it to someone. If we only knew who he saw in New York."

"I bet it is on the list," both men laughed. Rina looked up at Conrad at the same time as Wes turned back towards her. He moved into the light, smiled, pointed at Rina, and then ran his finger across his throat.

"Bye," he said, raising his eyebrows.

As soon as the door clicked, Weston whispered, "I know, but you got to trust me."

Weston waited until Rina fell asleep, then he got up and stretched. He walked around the room, checking his watch every couple of steps. After his fourth lap, the door opened.

"Sorry, I'm late. I was speaking with the Norton character again. He still swears that Rina and Moon knew nothing."

"I'm starting to believe him. Tangy can be stubborn, but at this point in the game, I think she would have given in, especially after..." Weston's hand pointed to the body attached to the monitors. He shook his head and looked back at his mentor.

"She'll be okay, Wes," Marty said, his wrinkled hand reaching out to touch Weston's shoulder. "We have the best doctors in the country here."

"I know that. I just wonder..."

"You two will be okay, too. Fate brought you back together, and she should be grateful you are on the case. She doesn't know how lucky she is," Marty said, letting out a boisterous laugh.

"Yeah, you want to tell her or should I because if you met Tangy…"

"I remember Tangy from junior prom. She was hell-bent on getting out of pictures, and you two were having a loud discussion about it in the driveway."

"I forgot you were there! Yeah, she hates to have her picture taken. That is one of the reasons I kept our picture on my screensaver. That was one of the few times she smiled and posed without inserting a middle finger."

"She does that in pictures?"

"Look at the prom picture carefully, or any of the others she is in. If the photo was set up…"

"I like her more now than I did before. Wes, how did you blow it with this one?"

"That seems to be the question of the hour. So did Norton say anything else?"

"Just that Jacko had access to the trunk a lot, and the list could be anywhere. I asked him about Rina having it…"

"And?"

"Possibility, but he couldn't say where. How many bags did she have?"

"That's the thing. Only two: the tape case and her backpack. I have been through both and even had the recorder taken apart…" He watched

Marty's lips turn upward, "Yeah, I knew it was a long shot, but I'm desperate here. Anyway, just electronics."

"Then it has got to be someplace obvious. What else was in the case?"

"Nothing. Recorder, blank tapes, batteries. She cut out foam inserts to fit all the components. We removed that too. Nothing underneath."

"Okay, what about the backpack?"

"Just what you would expect – clothes, tickets, toiletries, her journal." Weston stopped and looked up at Marty. Both men's mouths hung open. "You don't think?"

"Did you read it?"

"No. I figured it was just private thoughts and such." Marty raised his left eyebrow. "Okay, I started to, but a lot was incoherent, which I found amusing for someone who doesn't do drugs or drink, but I couldn't make heads or tails out of it, so I just stopped."

"We need to get the journal. Where is it now?"

"Everything is at my place in the spare room." Weston winked at Marty. "Should I…"

"No, I'll send a guy over. Third floor, right?"

"Yep. Her stuff is sitting on the floor by the bed."

Marty took a phone out of his briefcase and held up one finger to Weston. Without even a hello, he started, "Can we get a couple guys over to Traynor's place? Yep. They'll want to be on the third floor up in the loft space…" Weston watched Marty's lips form a huge smile. "That would be perfect. Let me know as soon as the party ends. Yep, thanks." The two watched Rina for a minute or two in silence. The reflection in the window of the observation rooms showed a quick stream of light. The door had opened, and their observer left.

"Okay, so where is her backpack, really?" Marty laughed. Their voices resonated a bit softer.

"In my trunk downstairs." Weston forced the return laughter. "Should I go get it?"

"If you don't mind," Marty followed Weston's eyes. "I'll stay with her until you get back."

"Thanks, Marty. Are you sure you want to be seen here?"

"It's okay. I got my guys everywhere, and we kind of just let the cat out of the bag, didn't we?" Weston nodded. He took one long look at Rina and started for the door. "Wes, no offense, but you may want to shower and change too."

"Yeah, maybe I'll do that." The door shut behind him.

Marty watched as Rina slept, wondering how one female cause could so much havoc in one operation. Rina had become a blessing and a curse. Weston had shifted his focus to keeping her safe, instead of the mission. Marty was going to have to fix that.

The tall, blonde nurse moved swift through the facility, flashing smiles instead of credentials. Luna wondered not for the first time why all the guards Marty used were male. A quick flash of her ample cleavage and a broad smile from her ruby red lips was all it took to get nodded past his troops.

She didn't look back at any point, although she knew their eyes would follow. She climbed the stairwell off a small corridor to an obstructed exit door. Getting in and out of the secure facility came was almost too easy. The security plans she had access to indicated nothing in the area, and she knew the layout of the building came from a reliable source.

"What have you gotten me into now, mother?" she murmured, and as if on cue, her phone buzzed. "I was just thinking about you," she smiled.

"Hopefully, good thoughts."

"Yeah, let's go with that. Where are you?"

"I was about to ask you the same."

Luna looked across the fenced area and cringed. Of course, she knew, "Walking the dog, what do you think?"

"Luna, what did you get from your friend?"

"At this point? Nothing, he was too drugged up to speak straight. He kept trying to tell me Doc was arrested."

"Oh, your other friend? We already knew that. We need to know where the list is if the patient wasn't speaking, increase the dose, I don't care."

"I can't go back, I'll get caught. Why can't you do this?"

"Because people know me. Why can't you just do as I say?"

"You know what, mother? When this is over, Wayback and I are getting married and leaving you losers."

"Oh, Luna, grow up. Wayback is not marrying you, and we all are moving to the ranch."

"You have no faith, mother."

"Luna, my dear, I have plenty of faith and much more experience with men than you. Please just do your job so we can all get out of here."

"Fine." Luna shut the phone down and let out a long breath. She began to laugh hysterically. Tears dripped down her cheeks while she clutched her stomach. She looked at the government issued portable phone in her hand. "This is crazy," she shouted. "Crazy!"

The authoritarian structure glared in the afternoon sun. Somewhere in that building, sat the key to this whole mess. Her mother or anyone of authority would never find it because Jacko didn't think the way they did. They were looking for something unique, and he didn't do special.

Luna pulled open the driver's side door with a little too much force. She stared between the wheel and the building, thinking about Jacko. The guy couldn't work a computer if his life depended on it, so a disc or other storage device was out. He had to use something bigger yet not noticeable.

She started the car and pulled out on the road, driving along the fence line. She had to talk to Cowboy straight, not drugged. That meant only one thing that Cowboy was expendable. Luna took in another deep breath. "That is just too bad," she exclaimed.

Cowboy's fate really wasn't her problem anyway. If he weren't hallucinating, he would figure out the connection eventually on his own. Cowboy could be semi-intelligent when sober. Luna slapped the wheel hard. Maybe he had already figured it out, and that was why they were keeping him in that place. He looked fine the last time she visited. Crap! Without being stoned, how long would it take him?

"This is all Rina's fault!" Luna screamed. "Why did she have to have a connection with my family, and why did she get involved?"

Once a trusted guard showed up, Weston moved down the hallway to the elevators. Doctors, nurses, and military personal acknowledged him with a smile or salute as he passed. With every address, he wondered whose side were they on. This situation made him suspicious of everyone around him, not a useful attribute for someone who depended on team effort.

As the elevator slogged up to the fourth floor, Weston's mind drifted through the leading players: There were Marshall Butman and his crew, they were the known factor. Beman and Mary were in the unknown, but there had to be someone else involved, possibly someone who Rina trusted.

The elevator door opened to another armed guard.

"Special Agent Traynor," he saluted. Weston returned the gesture and moved with purpose toward another guard, where even though they addressed by his first name, he still presented his ID. With a head nod, he entered the room where Neil Moon was sitting in bed, watching a cartoon with the sound off. The nurse on duty looked up as Weston sat in the closest chair.

"Can we have a minute?" he asked. Without a word, she got up and left. Moon turned toward Weston and then returned his gaze between the window and the cartoon. "How we feeling?"

"I'm ok. Are you going to press charges, or can I leave?"

"Interesting way to start a conversation with a friend of —"

"Yeah, I know who you are. Rina's friend, the narc, right?"

"I am Rina's friend, and I do work in law enforcement, yes. Narc? Only in specific circumstances."

"So the question remains," Moon continued, "when can I leave, or do I need a lawyer?"

Weston smiled at the lawyer's remark. Why did trust fund kids always think there was a buyout? "You don't need a lawyer, but feel free to call one. It's your dime. You will be released soon enough. First, we just have to make sure there are no after-issues from your overdoes —"

"I DID NOT OD!"

"Okay, okay. No need to scream."

"I'm sick of people saying that. All I did was look for some people, and the next thing I know, I wake up in a hospital bed. This is really messed up."

"Yeah, I get ya there. Can I ask who you were looking for?" Again the room fell silent. Weston watched Moon's eyes dart back and forth as Moon played Ping-Pong with himself on what to say and, more important, what not to say.

"A friend," he finally answered. "I was looking for a friend."

Weston waited for a beat then asked, "Did this friend have anything to do with Doc and the Asshole?" Weston saw a slight affirmation of his head. "Ok, can you share with me who?" Again Moon moved only slightly, shaking his head no. "Neil, do you mind if I call you Neil?"

"Are you really a friend of Rina's?" Weston motioned, yes. "You may address me as Cowboy, then."

"Okay, Cowboy, can you tell me who you were looking for? Rina already told me that she told you about Doc's arrest."

Cowboy's head moved to that invisible beat again, "Is this between you and me, because the other guys that were in here..."

"What other guys?"

"I don't know. There were a couple of buzz cuts that came around right when I was moved to this room. I got a little paranoid, you know because I thought they were the assholes from the bathroom, but they just asked a few questions and left. Still, I got the creepy vibe from them."

"Were they your only visitors?"

"Actually, no. I swear, my friend Luna was here. I might have been hallucinating because she was wearing a nurse's outfit, and she boogied on out of here after a little hallway commotion," Cowboy took a big inhale. "What was that hallway commotion, anyways?"

"Damned if I know. So this Luna person came to visit?"

"I didn't say she was real, but if she was, she kept asking about Doc and Rina."

"Do you remember what she asked?" A cold chill ran down Weston's spine.

"Actually, no. I thought she was a dream. I didn't pay much attention. You know Luna is a tour buddy and is always everywhere, so I figured maybe she was just here."

"Neil."

"Cowboy..."

"Cowboy, can you tell me more about the buzz cuts in the bathroom?"

"All I remember is that I was looking for my friend," emphasis on the word friend, "and there was a dude with bushy hair following me, so I slipped into the bathroom on the third tier. The friend I was looking for usually hangs out up there, and when I stood up, someone else grabbed me from behind and started asking questions."

"What kind of questions?"

"See, my other friend travels with a real asshole, and the questions were mostly about him… and Rina, I think. Yeah, I think they asked about Rina. That was when I freaked out and started swinging. I know I broke at least one nose, and then everything went dark, you know?" Weston thought back to one of his guys arriving at a meeting with two black eyes. He sighed. He would need Marty to pick him up too.

"Why do you call them buzz cut?"

"Cause when I was swinging, I connected with a few heads, and there was little to no hair. Otherwise, I would have grabbed and pulled." Cowboy shut his eyes. His body shook, but with a deep inhale, he relaxed. "So when can I go home?" he whispered.

"Soon," Weston replied back. "I'm telling you the same thing I told Rina and Bruce, is that his name?" Cowboy nodded. "For your safety, I need you to stay here for a few more days. I promise you can go home then." Cowboy went back to nodding to that invisible beat. "Could you do me a favor, and if your friend Luna shows up again, give me a call?"

Still, the beat continued.

"Thank you for your time," Weston got up to leave.

"Can you tell me one thing?" Cowboy spoke. When Weston didn't answer, he opened his eyes, saw him standing by the door, and continued, "Is all of this really because Doc gave a ride to an asshole?"

"It looks that way…"

"Unbelievable."

Across the street, a non-descript Ford Crown Vic with tinted windows was waiting for Luna. The back door opened, and she slid into Beman's arms.

"How'd it go?"

"Piece of cake. I did exactly what you said, and you were right," she said, leaning over to plant a kiss on Beman's waiting lips.

"Of course, I was right," he smiled. "Weston trusts me. I came from Marty's team."

"Don't get too cocky. They are both intelligent people, you know," Mary smiled at the couple in the back seat. "We still have to watch ourselves. What did you find out?"

"All business, no fun," the woman cooed back. Beman released her long wavy hair from the tight bun. Curls bounced around the couple, giving enough time for their lips to part and again taste each other. As they entered their own world, her head moved to provide visibility to the rest, and a loud cough interrupted their play. "Okay, fine," she pouted over Beman's ragged breath.

"Now, they think the list is in her journal. Do you think Jacko would have had access to that?"

"I don't see why not. Their stuff was always piled somewhere, and he did have the right to use of the trunk." Mary turned away from the young couple towards the driver. "What do you think?"

"I'm not sure," Marshall Butman answered. "Part of me thinks they are focusing way too much on Rina."

"But, she's on his screensaver…"

"He said she doesn't matter. Besides, why would Weston leave her with us if she did?"

"If it was me, I'd kill him," came a voice from the back seat. "You know, for leaving me with the bad dudes," she smiled up at Beman.

"Angel, you are not killing anyone, ever again…"

"I still might have to kill Cowboy if you guys fuck up again."

"I know darling, and that would too bad. It was unlucky that he knew you, but he hasn't mentioned you to anyone so far…"

"And we would know this how?"

"Because mama files all the team reports," Marshall Butman gaffed.

"Ah, so I have stumbled into a family business," Beman joked. "Back to the list…"

"Oh, yeah, they seem to think it is in Rina's backpack at Traynor's place. Should we head over there now?"

Silence filled the car while Beman's hand drifted up to his companion's thigh.

"I think we should send the boys over," Mary finally spoke. "Weston said he had a feeling he was missing something, so I would rather see caution and send expendables. Luna, you and Beman are not suspects, so we all just need to stay low key," Mary looked Luna in the eye. "That means no more trail mix for now." Luna rolled her eyes up to the ceiling. "I mean it, Luna. The trail mix worked for a while, but now that we are lying low."

"What about the people I owe?"

"Screw them," Beman chimed in. "This is about keeping our asses out of the slammer."

"He's right," Mary jumped in again. "We need to cut our losses and get out of here. Get the shipment and go!" She leaned in towards Meth Head Biker Dude, "You, darling need to stay off the radar for now and take my little angel wherever you go…"

"But, mom!!!"

"Yes, Luna, what have I told you about that? Butt and mom do not belong in the same sentence." Mary shook her head to refocus, "I will get the boys over to Weston's. I have a key to his place, you know," laughter erupted, "and we will meet up later."

"Should our guys be beefed up?"

"We may want to bring a few toys. Do we know who Marty is sending?"

"No, just that he said he'd take care of it. For all I know, Weston may be taking a ride there himself. I left after I heard that figuring, we would want to get there first."

"At least you are thinking," Mary watched Beman's hand reappear to rest on her daughter's knee. "Beman, you need to get back in there sooner rather than later."

"I was going to nap and shower then head back in a couple. Thought that…"

"Yeah, no. My daughter will not be joining you. Angel, go with Marshall for now, please. You two can do what you want after this thing is over."

"Like go to Vegas and get married?"

Mary watched Beman flinch at her daughter's words. "We can do a Vegas wedding if that is what everyone wants," Mary answered, continuing to study Beman's reaction. "If that is what everyone wants…" she glared into his eyes.

Weston walked to the observatory near Rina's room and took out his secure cellphone.

"Marty, there's someone on the inside here, posing as a nurse."

"Or the boy's hallucinating," Marty replied. Through the glass, Weston watched Rina sleep, her lips turned up into a soft smile.

"I don't think so. My gut—"

"Has been on so far. I'll tell the guard to be alert. What else did Moon say?"

"Not much. Everything points back toward Jacko, and it looks like the others were just along for the ride per se."

"Interesting. Oh, speaking of which, guess who we picked up at your apartment?"

"An agent with two black eyes, perhaps?"

"How did you—"

"Just found out that angle, Marty. It seems that Moon went down swinging. He also mentioned the folks who attacked him in the bathroom all had buzz cuts. He said there was no hair for him to grab on to."

"Buzzcuts as in military?"

"Not sure, but this kind of points that way. Military or law enforcement…"

"I guess today's round-up had some merit to it after all." Weston heard clanging on Marty's end. "Really, now? Anyway, we are getting closer to the center of this circle. Weston, I think you know what our next steps are."

"I'm heading over there now. I just wanted to check on Rina first. We should plan on moving her and Moon to the same floor after she wakes up."

"I'm hoping to have this wrapped up before that is necessary."

"Of course," Weston flinched. "Not sure what I was thinking. What about Norton?"

"Who?"

"The driver. Can we get him out of holding and maybe over here too?"

"I don't think that's a good idea, at least not yet."

"Just a thought," Weston nodded in the darkness. "Okay, well, I guess I will go and…."

"Weston, we are so close here. Let's just stick to the plan."

"No problem. I will call you after the meeting."

"Speaking of meetings, your team is more than aware of your relationship with Rina, but you might want to have a briefing of sorts."

"I have been, via phone. I didn't want to leave Rina or bring in more people than I had to."

"I understand that, yet you need to put up your façade and if this was any other case…"

"We would have daily briefings. You are right, Marty. I will have Mary set that up."

"Well, have someone else call it in. Mary was on the original arrest report, yet, she never made it to holding."

"You are just telling me this now?"

"Listen, Wes, I have someone watching her and a couple other guys we are trying to ID. They are hauled up near the docks. She seems to be our key to the shipment."

"I suspected that."

"So you understand that she was allowed to go her own way purposely and now is lying low. Between Mary and Butman, the inner circle should be revealed."

"I agree."

"And just to ease your worried mind, I will put extra guards on Rina and Moon during that time. Let me know how it goes today."

"I will, thanks." Weston placed his phone back into his briefcase and then picked up the landline. Without any greeting, he stated, "Mary, we need a staff meeting at four today to bring everyone up to speed."

Mary started to say why that was a bad idea, but stopped herself, "Weston, do you want the field agents too?"

"Thanks for reminding me. Have Beman there too. I want to go over the reports and make sure we are all on the same page.

"Will do boss." After hanging up, he left a message with Marty's secretary about the meeting time and place. Weston opened the door leading into Rina's room. The doctor monitoring the machines jumped, breathed deep, and acknowledged Weston with a head nod.

Weston reached down to take her hand in his. The smile on Rina's sleeping face grew. "I will be back soon, Tangy," he whispered as he leaned over to kiss her cheek. Rina let out a contented sigh.

Weston walked through the next set of security gates, knowing he would have to go back to the beginning. Loud metal clanging followed his every step. Long gray hallways led to a dull, lightless room with one table and two chairs. He wanted to meet in a more relaxed place, yet Marty advised otherwise. "You want the advantage here, Wes," he instructed.

The room smelled like the metal surrounding it. In the distance, a loud clanking signaled that his next interviewee would soon arrive. When the door opened to reveal a skinny, strung out kid, Weston was surprised. Jail had not been kind to him. The constant sneezing and the washed-out facial expression of an addict needing a fix suggested this meeting might be a waste of time for both.

"Jacko," Weston addressed the mess across the table.

"Who the fuck are you?" he spat back as he wiped his nose on his sleeve.

"A friend," Weston waited while he thought about this.

"Yeah, I don't think so. Who are you?"

"Friend of Rina's." A blank look came over Jacko's face.

"Who the fuck is…" His eyes grew wide. "The princess is a fucking narc!" he exclaimed.

"Actually she's not," Weston enjoyed the confused look this brought. "Rina is my friend, and I am a narc," he laughed.

Jacko bit on his lower lip while he watched Weston, relax across from him. He started nodding to a beat only he could hear, much like Moon but without the smile. Weston sat and smiled back at him, waiting.

"So you are a friend of Rina's," he nodded in Weston's direction. "Well, we all know how friendly Rina can be, don't we?" Weston leaned forward to rest his elbows on the table. His biceps contracted and released under his suit jacket. "Do you know Rina that well?" he asked.

"Most people do," Jacko met his stare and retreated to gaze around the room.

"She has an interesting pet name for you," Weston leaned back in his chair. He caught the guard's attention and nodded.

"I'm sure she does," Jacko cooed back.

"Yeah — it is the Asshole."

Jacko sprang across the table at the same moment the guard grabbed him from behind to slam his uncoordinated body back into the chair. His breath came heavy with minor convulsions ending with one arm slumped over the back and the rest of his body leaning to the side.

Weston signaled the guard who stepped back a few feet. "Now, can we talk?" he asked a little more aggressively than he tried to appear.

"Suit yourself."

"Jacko, you were traveling with a few associates, correct?"

"If you say so."

"I don't say so," Weston snapped. "I am asking you a direct question."

"I was traveling to shows with what I thought were friends."

"Okay, so are any of these 'friends…'" Jacko shook his head no. "Good. What did you have that is so important to others?"

"Nothing." The guard's shadow made Jacko jump. "Okay, something."

"We already know about the list," Weston watched Jacko hunch down further. "Can you tell us anything else?"

"Let me go, and I'll give you a copy," he sat up straighter now.

"I can't let you go, but we may—"

"You don't get it, man. I'm a dead man if I give that to you. Amazingly, Rina is still alive considering, everything. At least I am assuming she isn't dead yet." Weston took in a deep breath. "This thing is so big… too big. You can't stop it or control it. There are people high in the government protecting each other. Some you may know. There is a network out there that is unbreakable. There are heads of industry and so many other powerful people that this is beyond you and me," Jacko started to fling his arms. The guard did his best to avoid getting hit. Weston sat and watched.

"Do you know these powerful people?"

"Some, but I wouldn't rat on them. I've seen what they can do, and it is," Jacko's eyes watered, "it is not pretty."

"So it is prettier in jail?"

"At least I'm alive." Weston took a minute to think about this while Jacko wiped his nose again. His bravado left, and desperation seeped through his hunched body.

"We are done here," he nodded to the guard, who wrapped his massive arms around Jacko and helped him to a standing position.

"Hey friend," Jacko spat as Weston reached the door. "You would be surprised at who is involved in this. Watch your back."

Weston left without a word. The only clue Jacko gave pertained to Rina, and Weston didn't like where that was heading. His stride quickened through the holding area as he moved from the high-security area to offices. Ignoring the assistant out front, he ripped open the door. A short, thin man sat behind the desk.

"Up the guards on Jacko. I need to see the other one," Weston stated without greeting.

"And how is your day going?" the man replied as he picked up his phone. After relaying a few instructions, he turned back towards Weston, "Better?"

"Not really. Jacko is an…"

"Asshole?"

"Yeah," Weston replied with a smile. "Yes, he is."

"So your interview didn't go well, I take it."

"He has the information I need or at least knows where it is. This is frustrating."

"We can beat it out of him." The reply got a snicker.

"You are serious?"

"Of course not, but there has to be something Jacko wants."

"He is afraid, and he kept saying we couldn't control this. It goes too high."

"They all say that Wes," the assistant out front appeared in the doorway.

"You are all set," she stated and disappeared. The man behind the desk rose up and shook Weston's hand. "Good luck, and let me know what else you need."

##

Her room now had a couch in the middle with a glass coffee table surrounded by two winged back chairs in a brownish-gray color. The tiled floors running throughout the building were the only indication of a Unitarian facility. The soft, warm, gray tone on the walls even made the surroundings seem pleasant. Wes drank out of a plastic water bottle. As he waited, he thought about the many ways Rina would scold him for his beverage choice.

"There is a huge plastic garbage patch in the middle of both the Atlantic and the Pacific Ocean. The bottle is made from petroleum products. It will give you cancer. The water is

from a tap, so you might as well drink tap water."
She would probably add *you idiot* on to the last
one. Bruce walked in to find Weston laughing at
his water bottle.

"I don't think I should drink the water,"
he commented offhandedly. Although
disheveled, Bruce didn't look as bad as Jacko had.
Though he also had bags under his eyes and dull
skin, Weston attributed this to anxiousness rather
than drug withdrawal. "Bruce," he introduced
himself while extending his hand.

"Weston. We met before." Bruce brought
his hand under his chin, resting his index finger
across his nose and shrugged. "When you were
first brought in. I'm Rina's friend." Still, no sign of
recognition.

"I like Rina," he finally spoke. "She's a
good person. Is she okay?"

"Yes."

"Good, because I have been worried about
her. She disappeared when…"

"Yeah, I know. She is with me." Bruce's
eyes went dark as he squeezed his hands together
tight, then released. Weston watched and waited.

"So, Rina is a narc…"

"Actually, no. I'm a narc. Rina is the
wrong place, wrong time." Weston posed this
question. Bruce nodded his head. "That is what I
thought. Bruce, I'm here to help you. Somehow

you got mixed up with the wrong people," Bruce nodded, "and I want to make sure you don't get blamed for their shortcomings."

"That would be nice." He watched Weston smile and then added, "Do I need a lawyer?"

"We can get you a lawyer, sure, but I don't know if you need one yet." Silence. "Bruce, Rina is in trouble. It seems that some evil people think she has something they want."

"Like what?"

"A list of some sort," Weston waited, but Bruce's facial expression did not change.

"Jacko's list?" Weston nodded. "Why would Rina have Jacko's list?" Bruce's hands slammed down on the table, bringing a guard exploding through the door. "That asshole! I told him to stay away from her. What a dick."

Weston caught the guard's eye, and the guard automatically took a step back. In a voice much calmer than he felt, Weston continued. "Jacko may have left something significant that put Rina in danger—"

"I'd say. That, that, what a… I can't even speak!" Bruce's arms flew up in the air. "I tried to protect Rina. I had her stay at the hotel and wait while I took Jacko around. She didn't come out to any of the all-nighters that I know of…" Another slam on the table, "I should have left her home or made her travel with someone else." A blank expression ascended on his face, "I should have left her home."

"How did you meet Jacko?"

"Who? Oh, the Asshole," he chuckled. "He is a friend of a friend. She said he needed a lift to the shows and had cash to chip in for the trip."

"Did he?"

"Oh yeah—but he always needed to stop at this friend's houses to pick up the money they owed him or stop by his cousins who had cash or some..." Bruce glared at Weston.

"Some what?"

"I was going to say weed, but I didn't want to incriminate myself further."

Weston laughed. "Marijuana is not the issue here," he gestured with his hand to continue.

"Yeah, so we would stop here to pick up a little weed. I had no idea what he was actually doing until we got to the Bronx, and then it was too late. I planned on finding my friend in DC to try to ditch the dude, but..."

"Okay, so you figured it out. Then what?"

"You know the rest. We made a few stops on the way down, and the last one was where I got busted." He took in a deep breath. "I figured Rina took off because the girl has listening problems and most likely did not stay in the car as I told her to."

Both Weston and Bruce turned to the sounds of laughter morphing into a cough. "Sorry, sir," the guard nodded.

"My friend speaks the truth," Weston smiled back. "She has always had listening issues. When she got out of the car, I got her out of the situation."

"Rina is with you?" Weston nodded. "And she still has her backpack?" Again another head nod. "You need to get that backpack from her. She could get…"

"Killed?"

Bruce nodded. Weston took in a deep swallow of air then fixed his eyes on Bruce. "Rina is in a hospital bed fighting for her life right now," Weston chose his words with care as he continued. "Along with a friend of hers, Cowboy?"

Bruce gasped and put his hands on top of his head. He sucked in deep breaths. Droplets formed around his eyes as he looked up to meet Weston's. "I didn't mean…"

"But it happened."

"I really was going to…"

"Who is the friend that introduced you to Jacko?" Bruce hesitated. "It is either you or her at this point," Weston waited.

"I really can't."

"Okay, yes, you are going to need a lawyer. Make sure it is a good one too. Oh, and Barney, you can move him to a regular cell. I think we're done." Weston got up to leave as the guard stepped forward.

"Her name is Luna," Bruce whispered. "I don't know her real name. She travels with the bus people and sells hippy trail mix amongst other stuff on tour."

Weston sat back down. "Thank you. I am going to do my best to move you someplace other than here."

"Are Rina and Cowboy going to be okay?"

"They should be, but only time will tell. I should get her backpack?" Bruce nodded, yes. "Anything, in particular, I am looking for?"

"I'm not sure. I caught the Asshole reading her journal one night. Maybe that has something to do with it? I don't know. He was always going through her stuff, stealing her trail mix. She started to sleep in the tub with the bathroom door locked if we didn't have a suite. She said she got sleazy vibes from Jacko and didn't want to chance it."

"Smart girl."

"Yeah." Weston stood and reached over to shake Bruce's hand. Another guard walked in. Weston turned, recognized an ally, and instructed, "Take him to Marty's place please..."

"Do I need that lawyer?"

"Marty's place is more of a safe house than a prison. I think maybe Rina was right about you."

"Thanks."

Weston watched the three men leave. He took out a small notebook to jot down a few thoughts. He underlined the name Luna three times. He needed to check in on Rina and then head back to his office.

The puzzle was beginning to form.

Weston arrived back home in time for a quick shower and a change of clothes. He had grabbed Rina's pack out of his trunk and brought it up. In his kitchen, Weston pulled out each item and stacked it all neat on his counter.

Used concert tickets from a dozen shows created a map of where she had traveled in the past six months. Scraps of paper with scribbles of songs told the tale of what the band had played. He inhaled her scent off of a worn t-shirt with an embroidered rose and a giant curvy China Doll on the front. The smell of Rina made him light-headed.

Weston shook each garment before adding it to a pile on the floor. There was a bottle of patchouli oil, her toothbrush and toothpaste, shampoo, and a razor placed together in a plastic baggy. He shook the bag out to look at the crumbs of food and plants sitting on his counter. Nothing of use appeared.

The front zipper stuck, yet after a couple tugs, he got the other compartment open. A plane ticket home, her driver's license, a credit card, and some cash all meshed together into a glob. The only other object, her journal, and pen had a fascination and repulsion at the same time. He pulled out the small unicorn decorated bookstore notebook and placed it on the counter.

The pages appeared worn. She had been carrying this one for a while. Weston opened the book and untied the ribbon holding the used pages together. He flipped back to the first page. *I danced in the pine trees at Saratoga, yet something was off. I wish I could shake the feeling of being watched.* He smiled then continued reading, *the music is lovely and when I am dancing my life is perfect. It is when I stopped that things get weird. Spinning around arms stretching to the stars, wanting everything to remain the same....*

Well, la tee da... Doc took off to drive the asshole somewhere again, and I am left in the city to fend for myself. I walked from the Fairmont down to Times Square to take in all the lights and freaks. The city has an energy like no other. I met a few folks who were in town hanging out too. We went to some veg head restaurant and stayed until we were kicked out. So we headed to Wetlands to catch a really bad acoustic dude. He kept forgetting the words and would stop in the middle of songs to ramble about God knows what. Some folks just shouldn't smoke pot. It started to get a little strange, so I said good-bye, and I cabbed it back uptown. I got into the room just in time to lock my door.

Dipshit and Dimwad returned with a bunch of people in tow at 3 am. Doc slipped a note under my door that said, just sit tight – not your scene. *I would be really pissed if I wasn't fed and tired. I guess that is what happens when you travel with assholes. It is better than living alone in Alabama!*

So she did still think about him, Weston laughed at the last statement. When he turned the page, he stopped. Someone else's handwriting had inserted notes on the back of the entries. Rina made curvy, readable letters, while the notes had short and condensed lettering. In this fast scrawl, an address and a dollar amount appeared on the back of each page.

Weston grabbed the stack of concert tickets and a blank piece of paper. He flipped through the pages and wrote each address and amount he could find. Then he took each ticket stub and placed it next to an address that was close to a venue. A pattern started to emerge.

Each scribble coincided with a concert. In between the concert cities, it separated by a day or two. He sat back and smiled. The route mapped out before his eyes. Now all that's needed to complete the list is contact names. Weston tapped his pen on the counter. He flipped the pages to Rina's last entry. *God, my life is a mess. Here I am stuck at Weston's, yeah, that Weston's, because Doc and the Asshole got arrested. I would have been busted too, but Wes pulled me out of the mayhem. I guess I should be grateful. Tonight I couldn't even enjoy the show, and they played that blues jam that I love to dance to. I'm feeling like I'm in a B horror flick. You know, where the friends get arrested, and the main character is stuck in a really bizarre situation. Of course, some scary dude has to get in the picture to keep the plot going: enter Meth Head Biker Dude. Unfortunately, he is going to kill me, maybe Wes too, and that would suck. Not just Wes dying, I mean either one of us dying. My life is so strange!*

Maybe I just need to sit and meditate… or take one of those showers. Wes' shower is just like that one in Miami. God, I love that shower. Maybe it will wash away the mayhem, and I can go back to my normal semi-boring existence. Weston closed the book. She really wasn't as tough as she wanted him to think.

He tried to picture Rina here permanently yet had a hard time putting her in his world. Then he thought about being in hers. They would need to make compromises on both ends. But could they? Compromise was one area in which both lacked skill.

A knock on the door interrupted his thoughts. "Just a minute," Weston grabbed the list off the table and crumpled the paper into his pocket. With one move, he dropped the journal into a kitchen drawer and moved towards the door.

"Hey, Beman, what is going on?" Beman followed Weston inside.

"Nothing. I got your message to pick up Rina's stuff?"

"What message? I didn't call anything in."

"Huh, weird. Mary told me to swing by and get Rina's backpack." Weston reached down and handed the bag to Beman.

"Here you go, but there is nothing in it. I've been through it multiple times…"

"I don't know. Should I still bring it back?"

"Why not, maybe I overlooked something." Weston glanced at his wrist. "Is there anything else I need to know?"

"Still looking for the person who attacked that Cowboy dude and trying to figure out who else is involved. Got to tell you, boss, the trail is getting less visible as time goes on." Weston nodded. "Do you think we should talk to Jacko again?"

"Jacko, no, I just spoke with him today."

"Uh, boss…" Beman started towards the door and stopped short. "Should I go see him? I mean, I heard that he has been moved from our holding tank."

"He has? Since when?" Weston tried hard not to smirk.

"Don't know. I looked him up earlier and then asked Mary. She thought he was still downstairs."

"I need to make a call. Hold tight on seeing Jacko, ok, Beman? I'm going to see Rina, and then I will meet you all back at the office for the staff meeting. Take the backpack and let me know if you find anything." Beman nodded and exited. Weston sat back and laughed. He waited a few minutes to reach for the phone inside his briefcase.

Still laughing, he dialed, "Hey Marty…"

"You got a new joke, Wes?"

"No, it's just Beman was here looking for where Jacko is being stored. It took a lot to keep a straight face."

"What did you say?" A snicker in Marty's voice made Weston smile.

"Told him I needed to make a call and find out what is going on. He also said that Mary told him Jacko was moved."

"And you didn't tell Mary…"

"Not a thing." Silence fell between the two. Weston repositioned himself on the stool while he pulled the journal out of the drawer. "I got a few items to drop at your office for safekeeping, then I'll do a quick briefing."

"Now should we pick up Mary?"

"Not yet. Let's give her enough rope to hang herself. After all, the woman is not stupid."

"I agree. I'll put a tail on her, and maybe we can round up a few underlings too."

"What about the delivery? Are we set there? We got one shot, Marty…"

"I got my team moving in on the warehouse area in two days. So far, the only people outside the team who know the plan is me, you, and I gave Sal a heads up too just in case this all gets messy."

"Don't you mean, messier?" Weston laughed.

"Exactly. I don't want to take any chances. I'll see you in a few."

"Roger." Weston tucked the phone and journal into his briefcase. He grabbed an apple off the counter and headed out the door.

Luna smiled at the security guard outside of Cowboy's room then pushed the door open. Just as he had been when she left last, Cowboy sat in his bed, staring out the window.

"Just leave my lunch on the table," he turned toward the door. "Luna!"

"Shush," she moved in two steps to cover his mouth. "I'm getting you and Rina out of here before it is too late."

"I thought I dreamed you," Cowboy grinned.

"Yeah, I'm a vision." Luna pulled a pair of worn jean shorts and a tye-dyed shirt from her purse. "Sorry, no undies," she shrugged.

"How did you know I was here?"

"Long story. I need you to get dressed, and then we will go get Rina." Luna paced while Cowboy flung on the shirt and shorts. He stood and fell back on the bed. "You are going to be a little dizzy from sitting all the time. It will wear off." Cowboy went to remove his pulse monitor. "Oh, not yet," Luna instructed. She took a small box out of a purse and slipped the monitor from Cowboy's finger onto the box. Carefully she placed both in the middle of the bed.

"Now what?" Cowboy asked.

"Just follow me, and don't say a word, okay?" He nodded and stood behind her. Luna opened the door. The guard stood down the hall, flirting with the day nurse. Luna waved in his direction while she positioned Cowboy to walk the opposite way. They rounded the corner and entered an empty stairwell.

"Are you going to tell me what is going on?" Cowboy held the railing and moved awkwardly down the stairs.

"Not yet," Luna answered. "We need to get Rina first." Luna pushed open the door to the fourth floor and peeked out into another empty hallway. Everything appeared as her mother said it would. "Okay, now you need to stay close and quiet. We need to sneak into her room and then get out fast. Make sure Rina knows you are with me, okay?"

Cowboy nodded. They held on to the white walls through one empty hallway and into the next. Luna whispered, "Stay here. I will be right back," and she disappeared around another corner.

Cowboy slid down the wall and rested on the cold floor.

Luna nodded to several men in white coats. She stood tall and moved with a sense of authority that no one questioned. As she turned into the next hallway, she met the guard by Rina's door. It wasn't anyone she recognized, so she made a quick left and opened the door to the observation area.

She let out a long breath at the sight of an empty room. Through the window, she could see Rina sitting up in the adjacent room. Luna tilted her head to one side and stared for a minute. Rina looked so fragile, surrounded by blinking machines. With a deep breath, she opened the door leading in.

Rina moved her head in the direction of the click. Her eyes widened at the sight of Luna. She smiled, "Luna!"

With one swift move, Luna ducked behind her bed as the main door burst open.

"Ma'am?" a tall, athletic buzz cut entered.

"Yes," Rina answered. Her gaze focused on her guard.

"Sorry, thought I heard something…" He turned to the voice behind him. "Excuse me," he muttered as he backed out of her room.

"Do you have clothes here?" Luna popped her head up. Rina shook her head no. "Okay, try this one." Luna reached into her shoulder bag and pulled out a simple sundress. She then started to disconnect wires and reconnect each to a small box produced from her pocket.

"What are you doing?"

"Quiet! I'm getting you out of here. This is bad, Rina, really bad. I have Cowboy in the hallway, and we are leaving…"

"But how?"

"Just follow me. I have got you out of jams before, and I'm doing it again," Rina started to tear up as she caught Luna's eye. "Come on, man, do not do that," Luna whimpered. "We are friends. And friends take care of each other." Luna wiped the water from her face and then helped Rina up from the bed. She placed the black box in the middle of the mattress, then lead Rina into the side room. With arms lifted, the gown dropped to the floor as the black cotton dress slid over her body.

When Rina shook her head at the two-way glass, "Now that is creepy," she replied. Luna stopped and looked at her friend.

"Ri, things are going to get weird, but you have to promise me you will stick by my side and do what I say."

Rina nodded and then asked, "What about Wes?"

"I was waiting for that question. Weston Traynor isn't your friend, Ri. He left you with those hoodlums, and you had to escape on your own. You almost died, man," Luna threw her arms around Rina in a tight hug. "I'm here to save you both."

Rina hugged Luna back and took one last look at her prison. "Let's get out of here," she exclaimed as they broke the hug.

"Do as I say," Luna repeated again. Rina took a decisive step toward the door and allowed Luna to lead her through the halls. As they rounded the corner where Cowboy sat, Rina let out a short squeal. Luna's hand flew up to cover her mouth. "Quiet," she stage whispered. Cowboy walked his lanky body over and embraced Rina.

"You are such a drama queen," he choked out.

"Missed you too," Rina wept in return.

"Okay, you two, we need to move." Luna led the group to the end of the hall. An emergency exit sign with red flashing light waited. "Please, mother, come through," Luna whispered as she pressed the door open.

No sound came out. "Let's move people," she directed down the stairs. Their footsteps echoed in the silence. Luna pushed open the door at the bottom. The intense mid-day sun temporarily blinded them. A strong arm moved Rina as her eyes adjusted.

"Good job, babe," the voice sounded familiar, yet Rina couldn't picture from where.

"Sit right in the back, princess." Rina pulled her arm away. Cowboy already had sat in the back of the black cargo van. Wayback smiled. "Did ya miss me?"

Rina tried to break free, yet another pushed her into the vehicle. "What the…"

"Ri, please calm down. We don't want to drug you again," Luna smiled. Rina moved to the back of the van and sat down next to Cowboy.

"Hey now," he nodded wide-eyed.

"Yeah," Rina responded back.

The shouting started at the same time, the door closed. They could hear Luna arguing with Wayback and another unfamiliar voice.

"What do you mean they are in the van?"

"Yeah, I thought if we could get the two of them out of this place, they could tell us where the list is..." Luna recalled their escape. "So we snuck out the way mom brought me in last time. It was—"

"Are you freakin' nuts?" the other voice boomed. "You used the escape route." A loud bang echoed in the van.

"Oh crap," the driver exclaimed as he exited the vehicle. "You can't talk to her like that."

Without windows, Rina and Cowboy couldn't see what was actually going on. Bits and pieces of the argument leaked in.

"I thought I was doing the right thing. We need to move this along and get out of here so we can get married."

"Tell her," the new voice boomed. Something hit the side of the van. "Tell her now…"

"Yeah, Luna, dear. We are not getting married…"

"I know that voice," Rina turned towards Cowboy. "That's Wayback. He works with Wes." Cowboy nodded yet did not comment back.

"What do you mean we are not…"

"We are not getting married," the voice firmly stated again.

"But I… and I… You bastard!" Another loud boom against the van was followed by a gunshot. The two front doors opened. The van shook sideways as two bodies jumped into the seats. The vehicle jolted forward.

"Are you freakin' nuts?" The passenger asked the driver.

The driver turned his head to glare at his companion. Rina remembered the profile. Grilled Cheese Man was driving the van. "We are screwed," she whispered to Cowboy, who was resting his head back against the seat, nodding to his own beat.

"Not yet," he whispered back.

"It had to be done," the driver snarled back.

"I know more than you that marriage is not in mine and Luna's future, but that was no reason…"

"Think about it, we are in the clear now. Luna was our tie back to the organization."

"What about her mother?"

"Covered, and the Buttster too."

"Do I want to know?"

"Probably not. The less you know, the better. Let's just say that Luna's demise will set off a chain of events that will make us millionaires in Costa Rica while the others rot in jail." A sharp turn sent Rina and Cowboy into each other. "I need you to go back to your office and send this from our friend's email. Once that is complete, well, she'll be gone."

"And the Buttster?"

"She'll take him down with her, especially if she thinks he had anything to do with Luna's untimely death. I'll take care of that."

"What about," Wayback jerked his thumb towards the back of the van.

"I'll take care of them too. If they don't have the list… well," Grilled Cheese Man gave a sideways grin and laughed out loud.

The van came to a stop. Wayback jumped out. "I'll be in touch," he echoed as he shut the door.

"Well, kiddies, there will be no visits to the beach this time," the driver laughed as he merged back into traffic.

Weston sat back at his desk and waited. This part of the plan made him uncomfortable. Mary had shown up in the office and went about her routine. On the surface, nothing appeared to be wrong, yet something must be off if Marty's guys didn't arrest her. They put their trust in someone who he wasn't sure warranted it. His door stayed wide open, and periodically he watched Mary pace and peek back.

"Can I get you, anything boss?" She leaned against the doorframe.

"No, I'm good. Have we any new news at this point?"

"Not that I have heard, but it has been a while. Do you want me to make a few calls?"

"Thanks anyway, Mary," Weston shuffled the papers on his desk. "Can you take over the briefing? Just make sure everyone knows what is going on, okay?"

"What is going on?" She asked.

"Just go over what we have so far," Weston dropped a few papers into his briefcase.

Mary didn't move. "And if you hear anything you think I should know about, just get in touch." Weston stood, grabbed his coat and briefcase, and walked toward his assistant.

"It will be okay, boss," she gave his arm a squeeze.

"I sure hope so." Weston felt Mary's eyes follow him to the elevator. He turned in time to catch her, staring in his general direction. Weston hit the button for a floor below, and then when it stopped, switched elevators and punched the button for the top floor. He marched down the hall to drop down on the couch in Marty's office. Marty held up one finger as he barked, "Keep me posted," into the receiver. He slammed the phone down and smiled.

"What do you want first, the good or the bad?"

Weston watched the smile fade. "I'll take the good."

"Always the optimist. That's what I love about you, Wes," Marty rose to move to the chair next to Wes. "Okay," he leaned forward to rest his hands on his thighs, "Phase one went almost perfect."

"Almost?"

"Getting to that. That Luna person managed to get both Neil and Rina out of the hospital. We almost blew it switching guards, but

Connor thought on his feet and would not let his replacement into the room."

"How did he do that?"

"I don't know, said she was sleeping or something, it doesn't matter. So Luna was able to get both out, and Neil has the tracker with him. My guys are following his feed, and we got people positioned along their suspected route."

"All good there."

"Yes, all good on that end. However…"

"However?"

"Getting to that… we see they are heading to the docks, probably to the warehouse we've had under surveillance. I am waiting on Beman to confirm that."

"Good luck with that one."

"Yeah," Marty sat back and laughed. He leaned forward again, his smile vanished. "Unfortunately, there was a casualty. Luna was shot and killed outside the hospital. My guy said someone in the van, and she argued, and then he heard a gunshot. They got to her as fast as they could, yet she was dead already."

"Does Mary know?"

"I was about to ask you the same."

"She didn't seem out of the ordinary, so I would say no."

"According to the cameras outside, it was the driver. We have his picture being run through the computer and are waiting on a match."

Weston nodded.

"What do we do about Mary?"

"That is what I was going to ask you, do you want to tell her and wait for a reaction, or do we put it in a report? She is a suspect, but she has been with you for a while…"

"I'll go tell her," Weston started to get up. "She is a suspect, yet I owe her at least that."

"You're a good person, Wes."

"Doing a shitty job, right?"

"Doing a hard job that makes the world a better place." The two men embraced. "Good luck."

Mary looked up and smiled as Wes approached her desk. "Oh, hey boss, I thought you left…"

"I did," he glanced up at the ceiling and then back at Mary. She sat erect with a serene smile pasted on her face. Wes noted the smile did not reach her eyes. "Got a minute?"

Mary followed Weston into his office and sat across from him on the sofa. Her body stood straight and tense. Wes leaned forward, placing his arms on his thighs and holding his hands.

"This must be serious," Mary dropped the smile from her lips. Wes shook his head, affirmatively. "Is it Rina?"

"Sort of," Wes reached over to take Mary's hands in his. "I don't know how to say this, so I just will," he stuttered. "Rina and Neil were kidnapped from the hospital today," He studied Mary, "and there was a casualty in the process."

"Oh Wes, I am so sorry," Mary squeezed both his hands.

"So am I Mary, so am I," he sucked in a deep breath, "Mary, we believe it was your daughter, Luna."

"That is impossible. She… Tears came swift as Weston moved to place his arm around her convoluting body. "Was it one of your guys?" she looked up to glare into Weston's eyes. Mascara ran down her cheeks.

"According to surveillance, it was the driver of the escape van. They were both involved in getting Rina and Neil Moon out of the facility. We are trying to find a computer match now. We are doing everything possible to catch the persons who did this," Weston squeezed tighter. "As you know, Mary, no one messes with my team."

Mary pushed back to get a better view of Weston. Her face expressionless, she reached over to the table to grab a tissue. She smeared the mascara under her eyes and then wiped her nose, leaving a faint trail of black underneath. She repeated the process with a clean tissue getting most of the schemer off her face.

"You need me to make a positive ID?"

"Mary, we are here for you. Whenever you are ready, I will bring you to see the body."

"No!" Mary jumped up. "I'll go myself… or I'll call my nephew… I can…" Tears started again. Wes put his arm around Mary to pull her into a hug. "This is not what was supposed to happen," she mumbled against his chest. "Kids, they just don't listen. They never would listen." Mary pushed back again, wide-eyed. "I have to get to the hospital," she stated and turned to leave.

"Mary, I will get a driver."

"Weston, I need to do this on my own. Thank you for your offer. I will call down to the pool. But you," she pointed her finger at him, "need to catch the bastards who did this!"

"I will, Mary. I promise you that"

Mary nodded and then walked out the door. Weston could hear her half-whispering, half-weeping on the phone. The conversation was awkward to make out.

He waited for a beat to check on her. From his office doorway, he watched his assistant throw keys, tissues, and a small handgun into her purse. She stood as he took a step forward.

"My nephew is meeting me over there. Can I get a ride with you?" she sniffled out.

"Of course. I just need to make a quick call." Weston dialed up Marty, and quickly relayed the conversation and confirming the fact that Mary was carrying a concealed weapon.

"I'll have my guy waiting in the garage to at least disarm her."

"Thanks, Marty."

##

Weston and Mary walked across the empty garage, the only sound coming from Mary's heels clicking on the pavement. Weston's car had been moved to a more visible spot. As he climbed in the driver's seat, a man reached out and grabbed Mary's purse. She turned to fight him, but he took off in a sprint toward the staircase.

"Why aren't you going after him," she shrieked at Weston. He sat in the driver's seat still. "Wes, what is wrong with you?"

"Get in the car Mary," he instructed. Another agent came around the corner and escorted Mary to the backseat. Mary didn't put up a fight as he slid in beside her. "Pretty shitty saying my daughter is dead, Weston. That is really low, even for you." She folded her arms across her chest.

Weston turned and watched Mary for a second before he spoke. He inhaled deep, "Mary, I am so sorry for your loss," he started to say. "Yet, I have to ask if you have any information about Rina's whereabouts. I would appreciate it if you told me now."

"Is Luna really dead?" Weston nodded. "Wes, I don't know anything except that my baby is gone."

"Mary, there is more to the story, and you need to help me."

"I know nothing and would like to call my lawyer."

"Do you need a lawyer, Mary?" He waited for her response. When she didn't speak, he continued, "Here is what I know. Your daughter was seen sneaking both Rina and Neil Moon, who were under my watch, out of a highly guarded military hospital." He waited for a beat and watched Mary. "She is not a government employee and had to get the layout and guard schedule from somewhere. Do you know where she got this information?" Mary still gave no response. "Mary, you have been with me since the beginning. I am not sure what is going on here, but I want to help you. You have to trust me."

Mary sat still and stared out the window. "Trust?" she quivered. "If we have trust between us, then what is with Twiddle Dee here?"

"I'm glad you asked. The surveillance camera system in the office scans for employees carrying firearms. I got a notice that you had a handgun in your purse and did not have the authorization to carry," he sighed. "Mary, if you feel threatened, I can get you that authorization. I just want you to be safe."

Mary watched her boss for a minute. Her legs stopped moving, and she uncurled her arms. "Thank you, Wes," She sighed. "I just thought I needed a gun because my daughter has been," tears dripped down her cheeks, "my daughter…"

she howled. Wes reached over to squeeze her hand and handed her a tissue with the other. His back dug into the steering wheel.

"Mary, come sit in front. Sergeant, I think…"

"Sir, I don't mean to be disrespectful. However, I am to accompany you both to the hospital. I have your clearances."

"I understand yet…" Mary got out, stretched, and then walked around the car. Weston watched every move. Once she got settled in the passenger's seat, Weston took both her hands in his, "Mary, the sergeant here has our credentials and such. He is going to help us cut through any bureaucracy and get to where we need to be, is that alright?" Mary stared at the floor and nodded yes. "Good," Wes placed her hands in her lap and started the car. He met the other man's eye in the rearview mirror to give a slight nod. The gesture was returned.

"Cowboy, what are we going to do?" Rina cried. Her body covered in sweat as she and Neil rocked into each other.

"Don't you worry, Tangerina. Or is that name special for your narc man?" the driver taunted, shrieking with laughter. "Does he call you that because you're juicy?"

Neil put his hand over Rina's mouth and shook his head to quiet her. The van pulled to the right and ascended a spiral ramp, abruptly coming to a stop, sending Rina and Neil toppling onto each other. The door slid open, and Grill Cheese Man erupted in laughter.

"You wannabe hippies crack me up," he giggled. "Anyway, our adventure is ending here as I have a boat to catch." His body took up the whole door space, "I need the list, Rina. That list has names on it, including mine, along with dates and places I need to visit. I have gone through what's his name's car, Weston's place, Jacko's and your buddy's backpacks, and the only other place I can figure the list is on one of you."

"We don't have it," Rina blurted out. "You are not the first to ask."

"Then who does?"

"I don't know. I just got a ride to a few shows with someone who I trusted like an ass, and now I'm here with you. I have been shot at, kidnapped, put in awkward situations, and watched good friends die."

"She really wasn't your friend, by the way."

Rina silenced her rant to watch Grilled Cheese Man. "Yes, she was," she whispered as Grilled Cheese Man gushed into laughter.

"How do you think you got here?"

Rina stared for a beat before she started ranting again. "And now I am stuck here in this gross van while people are still asking about the same stupid list I still know nothing about."

"That is just a too bad lady because now you and your buddy can hang out with Luna and watch a Hendrix/Joplin concert live. If you are really lucky, maybe Bob Marley will show up for a jam or two."

While Grilled Cheese Man laughed at his own joke, Neil's foot connected with his head. Neil jumped to pull back the door and hit Grilled Cheese Man a second time. Neil grabbed Rina's hand and pulled her out of the van as their kidnapper lay in a clump next to the passenger door. Neil ran toward the nearest exit, pulled it open, and dragged Rina through. She tripped down the stairs trying to keep up with his long strides. At the end of the hallway, there were three doors. Neil went to push the first, but Rina pulled him back and pointed.

A red bar warned the alarm would sound if the door was opened. Footsteps and a door slam echoed in the stairwell. Neil yanked the door to his left open. A littered grass field separated them from a highway and the water. There would be no cover in this direction.

Rina yanked open the third door, which led down another dark staircase. Neil pulled her through as the footsteps resonated above. Down they sprinted into a dim-lit tunnel. Silver light surrounded them as they moved into the darkness. Neil stopped short and listened.

Silence. He placed his hand over Rina's mouth and nodded no. They walked together further into the twisting space. Small lights lined the area yet she couldn't see more than twenty feet ahead. They walked at a good pace, stopping every few minutes to listen.

"So far so good," Neil whispered. Rina looked down to see their hands entwined. "Stay close. We still need to be quiet." They moved further into the unfamiliar, descending further and further from where they came from, on a downward slant.

Rina's legs wobbled, and her breathing became audible. She pulled back on Neil's arm. "I have to stop for a minute," she whimpered. Neil nodded, and they stopped to lean against the wall to catch their breath. Their bodies cooled against the metal. "Where are we?"

"I'm not sure," Neil answered. "Away from the garage, I know that much."

"Are we safe?"

"Rina, your guess is as good as mine." He looked around the area. "I think we should keep going and see where this leads. That dude isn't stupid. If he can't see us in the field or hear us in the garage, he'll be down here eventually."

"We need to find a way out." Rina concurred, moving to her feet.

"We should get going," she indicated in the general direction. She pulled Neil up, and they headed further down. The tunnel twisted and began to slope upwards. As their steps got steeper, Rina's hand held Neil's tighter. They moved into a more lit area, still without a way outside.

"Fuckin' Doc," Neil chanted as his free hand skimmed the metal. "This is all his fault, you know."

"Well, his, the Asshole… and Luna."

"Yeah, about Luna."

"Not a good person, huh?"

"Not entirely sure there. She was a good person, but something happened. Maybe her boyfriend, something else, but the last couple of times we hung out, it was weird." Neil turned into another endless space. "Crap!"

"Cowboy, let's keep moving. Tell me what was weird."

"She was just different. Not as mellow. Jumpy, I guess. I don't know, she wasn't herself, and she kept looking around for her boyfriend and got really pissed when she couldn't locate him." He stopped and stared at Rina,

"It was like she lost herself when she became his girl."

"I don't know, you are being girly again, come on, and let's move," Rina smiled. Finally, her favorite Cowboy whom she waged war with had surfaced.

Another bend in the tunnel brought the paint to another decision. Two tunnels split off to the right: one lit, and the other in total darkness. A door beckoned then from the left, and in front of them, another staircase pointed down.

Cowboy studied the doorway while Rina ventured a few feet into each tunnel. "I think we should head this way," he pointed off to the left.

"Why?"

"I don't know," he threw his hands up. "What do you think?"

"I agree with you," Rina started to walk into the dark space. Cowboy grabbed her arm.

"You sure?" Rina shrugged and then pulled him into the tunnel. Once their eyes adjusted, the area wasn't as dark as thought. Rina led while Cowboy followed slightly behind. Their shoes grew moist as they progressed. As another fork came into view, but this time, the choice was already made for them.

To their left, there lay a dim light in the distance. To the right appeared vast emptiness. "I'm heading toward the light," Rina declared. This time Cowboy just followed along to what turned out to be an open door.

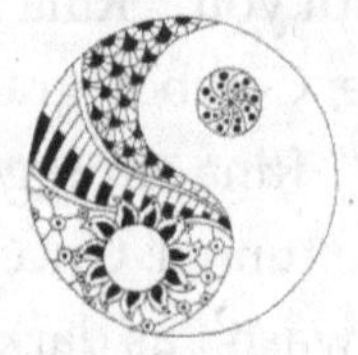

Mary twitched in the passenger seat as the car pulled up to the hospital. Upon arrival, their escort split off without a word, while Mary and Weston headed to the basement. Several gurneys covered with the outlines of humans lined the back wall. A uniformed officer stood in the doorway.

Weston flashed his badge as Mary stood behind him, focused on the patterns of white sheets and shiny metal. A small woman in a white lab coat fluttered out of a side room.

"Oh, Commander Traynor, I wasn't aware you had arrived," she reached out to shake his hand and gave Mary a quick head nod. "So sorry for your loss," she mumbled as she led them over to the far gurney. With a closer look, Weston saw spatters of red across the middle. He turned in time to catch Mary before she hit the floor.

"This one is a little queasy?" the tech inquired as she brought an inhaler from her pocket and waved it under Mary's nose.

Her eyes trembled open as she whispered, "Is it her?" Weston brought his gaze to the white sheet the tech had positioned to reveal the face of the deceased. Luna's eyes stared back into Weston's. Her lips curved into the smile of the all-knowing. Weston focused again on Mary and nodded his head yes.

The scream that escaped brought the guard running in with his 45 drawn. He watched the gray-haired woman hug the spattered white sheets, dampening the cloth with her tears. The commander stood back, watching the woman as she wept. He nodded to the guard, "I got this," and pointed back towards his post.

"Mary, I'm so sorry," Weston whispered. The lab tech had vanished back into her office as the two hovered over the body. "We will find who did this."

Mary stood to look intently at her boss. "I got this," she responded without emotion. "I got this," she murmured.

Weston placed his arm around her shoulders and moved her toward the door. Weston hit the button for the third floor to bring Mary into one of the grieving areas. The hospital was designed with small chapels scattered throughout to give family members a place to reflect. He sat Mary in one of the large comfortable chairs and started to sit in another one nearby.

"You don't need to stay," she spoke softly. "I would actually like to be alone for a few minutes."

"Are you sure?"

When Mary nodded, Weston reached over to squeeze her hand. "I'll be down the hall if you need me."

Mary waited for Weston to shut the door before reaching over for the phone. She picked up the receiver and listened for a beat before dialing. The soft clicking noises were almost inaudible. She stood to pace while counting the rings. One, two, three…

"Hello?"

"It's me."

"Why are you calling from this line? Is it secure?"

"Luna is dead." Mary's voice appeared barely a whisper.

"What do you mean?"

"What do you mean, what do I mean? She's dead! Shot!" Mary burst into tears as her voice rose.

"Traynor?"

"No. That is why I am calling you. I want to know who did this now!"

"Luna was supposed to stay low until we were ready to get her out of here. How did this happen? Where are the others?"

"That is what I want to know. They took Rina and Moon. Supposedly Luna led them out of the hospital via the escape route. Someone unassociated with the facility shot her in the parking lot and then took off with the other two."

"Did you get a look at the security tapes?"

Mary held the phone back and blinked twice at the receiver. "I've kind been trying to cope with my daughter's death." Mary twirled the phone cord and waited. Her hands shook. She stood and then sat again. The clicking noises became more prominent. "I need to get out of here."

"I'll call Beman to come to get you. Does he know?"

"I've been wondering the same thing. I don't think so because he would be here, right?" She could hear instructions being handed out in the background.

"Go to the public entrance, and she'll meet you there. Traynor may be with her, so be low key. Yeah, GO NOW!" The phone banged in her ear. "Okay, Mary, Winebox is on his way. Make up a relative, whatever. I'm going to try to find Beman and get him here. We can all meet at the warehouse."

"I can't leave Luna. I need to take care of her."

"Mary, I understand," his voice softening, "and I am sorry, but we need to get you out of there. I have a feeling…"

"Me too," Mary whispered back. She watched the door open, and Weston's form filled the frame. He hesitated before entering. "I'll call you back," she spoke a bit louder than intended. Weston sat on the chair opposite and slid a photo across the table that confirmed Mary's suspicions. The grainy frame depicted Beman, Luna, and a third man clearly. The third person aimed a gun at her daughter.

"I wasn't surprised to find Beman in the picture. Do you know the shooter?" Mary nodded yes but did not speak. "We got the whole thing on tape and are in the process of doing a facial recognition search."

"There is no need. He worked with us, in the agency, a few years ago," Mary said. "I didn't know Beman had been recruited too." She watched her boss. Her left hand moved into her purse, while her right blocked the view.

"Apparently he has. We also have him on camera sitting at your desk. This email," Weston slid another two pages across the table," was sent from your computer about ten minutes after we left. The timing works that he went from here directly to the office." Mary scanned the email.

Sent from her account to Marshall Butman, it outlined Rina's kidnapping and their next steps. Mary cringed at the last sentence: *Then we are free and clear to Vegas for the wedding.*

"Has he been picked up yet?"

"No."

"Why not? He is an accomplice to murder!"

"Because Rina is still out there, and he knows where she is."

"But, he murdered my daughter!"

"Mary, I'm sorry…"

"I called my nephew to come and get me. We need to make arrangements."

"Mary, please believe me. I will find this person and make sure he is punished to the full extent of the law, and possibly beyond."

"Thank you," she whispered.

"We are a team. We take care of the family." The door opened, and two military police filled the space. "I thought you would feel more comfortable having—"

"NO!" Mary shouted. "No, I am fine. Well, as fine as one could be." She watched Weston wave off the two visitors. "Weston, as I said, my nephew should be here any minute. I'd like to go home, notify the family," she looked up. "Do whatever one does when…"

"I understand." Weston stood and offered a hand. "I'll walk you downstairs."

Back in Marty's office, Weston slumped on his couch.

"You alright, son?"

"Yeah, I'll be fine. It's just hard when you work with someone and then find out they screwed you over."

Marty laughed. "I know what you mean. We put a tracker on her 'nephew's' car to follow her whereabouts. Do you think she knew the phone was tapped?"

"Probably, why?"

"Well, the folks over in the beach area are reporting hyped up activity, and her phone call went to one of the surrounding buildings near the warehouse."

"Interesting."

"Very. We also have eyes on Butman." Weston sat up straight.

"Say again?"

"You heard me. Visual ID has been confirmed."

"Why haven't you picked him up?"

"We are moving in that direction as we speak, yet we wanted to try to get Neil and Rina along the way."

Weston nodded. His foot began to tap, and he rubbed his chin. He shook his head no. "Marty, we have to get him. I love Rina."

"' Bout time you admitted it."

"And I want her safe…"

"But?"

"There is a bigger picture."

Marty watched Weston fold and then unfold his hands.

Marty shook his head no.

"Wes, we got good authority that if we bust Marshall Butman now, we miss the big picture. You know we have to go for the person in charge, and I don't think that was someone on your team." Weston nodded. "I appreciate you were putting the team first, yet let's do what we need to do to break the case, get Rina back, and then we will get Butman."

Weston went to stand, but his legs gave out. He gave a crooked smile and repositioned himself to stand. Marty shook his shaking hand. "Let's finish this. I need a vacation."

Rina held up her hands to shield her eyes from the blinding sun. Black dots appeared as she waited for everything to adjust. Cowboy stood behind her, taking in the pungent air and desolate field they were now a part of.

The parking garage sat about fifty feet away. Underground, Cowboy thought they had traveled further. He pressed the button on the side of his watch twice. Rina had moved about five feet from the door.

"Rina, stay close." He pulled her back toward the building. In a wave of rising heat, both could barely make out a vehicle coming across the sparse field. Rina looked back at Cowboy, who just smiled. As the SUV got closer, Rina noted the green camouflage of a military vehicle and relaxed a little.

"I think we are going to be okay," she smiled back at Cowboy.

"I think so too," he muttered in return. She turned and stepped back as the visitors approached. Cowboy tightened his grip on her upper arm, leaving imprints of his fingers in her biceps.

"What the hell, Cowboy?" She shuttered as a familiar voice filled the air.

"Nice job, Mr. Moon," Meth Head Biker Dude bellowed as he reached out to take Rina's right arm. She balled her hand into a fist and snapped it back around, connecting with Meth Head's jaw. He laughed thunderously. "Really?" he bellowed, jerking her arm again. "That's all you got?" She lowered her head and turned away.

"Cowboy?" The tears filled her eyes. He wouldn't even look in her direction.

"Rina, I had to do something…they were going to charge me with drug trafficking!"

"What happens to Luna?" Meth Head asked. Another man had stepped up and started to lead Rina towards the car.

"She got shot," Cowboy replied. He focused on the gun attached to Meth Head's belt.

"I know she got shot, you idiot! By who?" he bellowed back.

"I'm not sure. There were two guys, one Luna kissed and another one she argued with. The driver dropped the kisser off in front of a building a couple blocks away from the hospital. We escaped from the driver, who, by the way, is bat shit crazy."

"We are all bat shit crazy," Meth Head Biker Dude laughed back. Cowboy watched the gun come out of the holster. "Neil, I need to ask you a question," Cowboy nodded. Meth Head's voice had mellowed again, "There is a list that Jacko had. Rumor has it that he left it with Rina, but none of my guys can find it, and if Traynor had it, we would know, and we would all be in a different predicament currently."

"Yeah, I know nothing. Rina had nothing on her except the clothes she is wearing, and I think those came from Luna. I just want to get out of here." He hesitated then added, "She'll be alright, right?"

"Who, Rina? No, she won't be alright. She either gets us that list, or she will die." Meth Head replied as if he was giving his recipe for Luna's trail mix. "Yeah, unfortunately, I can't leave a trail because you know Traynor and how he is." Meth Head nodded at the man standing just behind him, who stepped forward to grab Cowboy.

He jerked both arms back before stating, "You got me in the face, last time dude. That is not happening again." Cowboy recognized the voice from the men's room. "My partner got busted by the Feds too!"

"Take him in the tunnel, and if you find the other idiot, bring him to me. We can let Mary handle that one, and I guarantee it won't be pretty." The man pulled to force Cowboy through the door.

Rina watched from the jeep while Meth Head Biker Dude and the Cowboy had what appeared to be a civil conversation. She observed the other man take Cowboy back into the tunnel, while Meth Head strolled back towards her. Her stomach curled, watching him speak to her guard as she waited.

The open door let the heat inside as both men entered. Neither spoke. Meth Head sat in the passenger's seat while his accomplice started the jeep and headed back across the field.

As Rina watched the garage fade away, she said a silent prayer for Cowboy.

The only sounds came from the hum of the air conditioner and the transmission changing gear. The driver opened the gate of a white brick warehouse complex with the push of a button. They followed the narrow path down the middle of the two buildings. In the end, the jeep took a hard left and parked on the side of a massive metal building. Rina could see it straddled the water with a rather large-sized boat inside, hidden from anyone's view.

The driver came around to help her out of the vehicle. With a brisk pace, he led her back into the brick building. She kept pace through the empty room. Through another door sat a small comfortable office and on the couch sat Mary.

Rina ran over and threw her arms around the woman. "I am so happy to see you," she gushed. Then Meth Head sauntered over and lowered his lips to hers.

"Hello, darling," he whispered. The other man lifted Rina off the couch, and her body replaced with Meth Head. He put his arm around Mary and held her whispering, "I know, baby. I am so sorry," as Mary sobbed into his shoulder.

"Can you give us a minute," he instructed, and another man pulled Rina into an adjoining room, that boasted just a few chairs on a concrete floor.

"Make yourself at home. The bathroom is in there," he instructed, pointing towards another door. He disappeared back through the door, followed by a loud click follow. Rina peeked into the bathroom, noting the sink, toilet, and no windows. She then tried to lift one of the chairs without any luck, so instead of continuing to pace, she plopped her body down into it.

As her adrenaline faded, she took deep, rhythmic breaths and sank into another world.

The ponytailed girls dressed in soccer shorts and tie-dyed t-shirts reached out to take Rina's hand. With one brown-haired cherub on each side, they skipped through the meadow of purple grass and silver sunshine toward the forest of tall green trees wrapped in orange flowers.

One child dribbled a soccer ball while the other carried a baseball bat with a glove on end. Both brown-eyed girls smiled and giggled as they went. Rina looked down at her simple purple cotton tank dress and the two small hands attached to hers.

"Mommy, can we go to see daddy now?" the baseball player asked.

"Why not," Rina shrugged. "This is better than purple teddy bears." Both girls laughed.

"Mommy, you are so weird!" the soccer player exclaimed.

As the trees grew closer, the orange flowers turned into small fruit hanging from the vines. A male form appeared sitting on a blanket underneath the tree.

"Daddy!" the two girls squealed with excitement. They dropped Rina's hands to run toward the man, waiting with outstretched arms. As his head turned toward her, she felt a nudge in her shoulder. His face came into a fuzzy view, while the smell of cigarette breath filled her nostrils. Just as the figure began to come into focus…

"Rina!" The voice made her jump from the chair.

"Where? What? Shit!" Meth Head Biker Dude and Mary's faces came into clear focus. She shook her head and took in deep breaths. Her hands started to shake while a strong push to her chest forced her body to fold back into a seated position. She sat back and looked up at both her captors.

Mary's eyes appeared bloodshot, and she had lines going down her face. Meth Head, still scary looking, had tears in his eyes too. Both seemed to need an extended vacation. Rina squeezed her eyes shut and then refocused. She could hear her breath intake as she waited. Finally, Mary spoke, "We have to talk."

Cowboy felt the sharp steel rod in the middle of his spine as his captor lead him back into the dark tunnel.

"We are going to have some fun," he heard the man whisper. He followed that with low laughter. "I am going to take you to places you have never been to. And after, I get to go on vacation in Costa Rica and park my fat ass on a beach and drink tequila all day, while you rot away in this tunnel. You see, my friend," he shoved the steel rod harder; "You are going to pay for Luna. Pay for what you did. You and that bitch my friends have. They are all going to pay…" He laughed again.

"What did I do?" Cowboy sniffed out.

"Be a man!" His captor shouted back. "Real men don't cry. Even when their sister has been murdered by a lazy ass."

"I'm sorry for your loss."

"Are you?" he screamed as he turned Cowboy around and looked him in the eye.

Cowboy noted the clenched jaw and bug-eyed expression as he leaned his body back. "You killed my sister."

"I didn't kill anyone," Cowboy pleaded. "I watched someone shoot a good friend today, that is all."

"THAT WAS MY BABY SISTER," His captor wailed. As he raised his arms to strike, Cowboy pushed forward to connect the shoulder to the chest. His captor fell back, and his gun discharged, but Cowboy twisted out of the way. He raced down the tunnel into complete darkness, while he could hear heavy breathing follow from behind.

"I am going to kill you," the voice echoed. "And then I'm going to torture you and kill you again for my Luna."

Cowboy stopped and breathed in deep. "Holy shit," he exclaimed as he forced his body to move. In the distance, a crack of light came into view. He just had to make it there before this crazy person rounded the corner.

The banging noises behind him started to fade as a stream of light bounced around him. Cowboy pressed his body against the wall and moved as quick and quiet as possible. The middle of the cavern was filled with stagnant water, which gave away his pursuers' position.

He sprinted through the fork toward the darker option. As he disappeared, a large mass blocked his movement, and a hand covered his mouth.

"Do not move or speak," the person whispered.

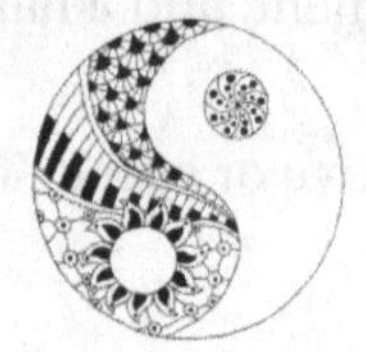

Rina nodded her head as Mary continued. "Did you see who killed Luna?" Rina nodded, yes. "Was it Beman?" Rina nodded, no. Mary took a deep breath in and looked over at Meth Head, who shook his head for her to continue. "I need you to confirm who killed my Luna…"

"Grilled Cheese Man," she stated with confidence.

"Who the hell is Grilled Cheese Man?"

"He brought me terrible grilled cheeses when I was held at the beach. I don't know his name, just that."

"Okay, can you tell me why did he shoot Luna?"

"Because Wayback or Beman, whatever, said something about murder not being a proper way to call off a wedding."

"Did he say anything else?"

"Grilled Cheese Man gave him instructions. He said something about sending an email and going to Costa Rica. I don't know because, at that point, I was more worried about other things."

"Grilled Cheese Man, huh?" Meth Head nodded.

"Who is that?" Mary asked. At Meth Head's stare, Mary's hand flew up to her mouth. "Are you kidding me? So the photo Traynor showed me bore the truth."

Mary rose and began pacing the room while Meth Head kept an eye on Rina. Mary would stop mid-step, turn, look at Meth Head, and then shake her head no. "We can't do that now," she sighed.

Rina watched the dance. Her focus wavered between Mary and Meth Head. Mary rambled as Meth Head watched. His eyes grew misty. Rina tried to make herself as small as possible, squeezing her knees up to her chest while she wrapped her arms around her shins. With the door too far away for escape and two bodies between it, she had to sit tight.

Rina thought she could take Mary out with ease, but Meth Head had the size and ability to break her with one swing. Tears dripped down her cheeks, some were for Luna, and some for Cowboy as she prayed for his safety.

Rina wept for herself too. Freaking, Wes had promised to keep her safe. And for the second time, he didn't seem to be. After the first time, he said he would love her forever, well that didn't work out so well. Now, here it was years later, and he was still nowhere to be found.

Finally, Rina had to ask the question she feared the most, "Are you going to kill me?" her voice quivered.

Both stopped pacing to look over in Rina's direction then at each other. "Are you going to kill me?" she asked again, her voice a bit stronger.

"Should we?" inquired Mary. She crossed her arms over her chest, tapped her left foot, and waited for an answer.

"Wish you wouldn't," Rina responded. "I mean, think about it. If this is all about making Weston Traynor's life miserable, wouldn't you want to let me go?"

"Why is that?" Mary asked.

"Because right now, I could kill him. I mean seriously, how many times can this guy leave me in a bad place?" Meth Head looked back at Mary and shrugged. "You don't believe me? The last time Wes and I hung out, he wanted me to move to Alabama! Alabama! And then," Rina started to fling her arms in the air, "this is the clincher now. Weston was leaving for God knows where within a week. So we would have moved there—"

"And then he would have left you?"

"Precisely!"

"Just like he left you with the kidnappers," Mary added.

"And how he said he would keep me safe, and I don't know about you, but I really don't feel so safe."

"It is always about Wes, isn't it?"

Rina shook her head. Her breath came deep. "Do you know where the list is?" Rina shook her head no, "Or what Weston knows?" Again she nodded. "Well, then what good are you?" Meth Head's burst of laughter made Rina jump. Mary turned towards Meth Head, "We can dump her off the boat. In the meantime, just keep her in here, and maybe she'll come in handy for something."

Mary walked out of the room. Meth Head looked at Rina, mumbled something she couldn't understand, and then followed. After the door closed, Rina stood and stretched. She walked the perimeter, stopping only to open the bathroom door. Two doors, no windows, only one way out, she repeated to herself.

In the next room, she could hear Mary and Meth Head yelling at each other. She couldn't make out what the argument was about, yet she tried to get the gist.

"Luna's body…"

"It is too dangerous."

"I don't care."

"We need to find…"

"Nooooo!"

Rina went back to the opposite corner as the door flung open. Meth Head took her picture and then slammed the door shut.

"Happy?" she heard him yell.

Weston looked at Cowboy's crumpled body, muttering "dumbass," to his colleague. In the distance, they could hear his stalker stumbling through the tunnel.

"I'll get you, you bastard!" he screamed. "Shit! Damn." He collided with something in the dark.

Weston held up one hand and counted off to five. Another agent took a rock and threw it down the tunnel that ran closest to where they stood. The clanging sound echoed.

"I got you now!" the voice came closer. Again, holding up his hand and counting off until five, Weston waited until the footsteps appeared outside their door. He dropped his arm at the same time two men jumped on top of Cowboy's assailant.

"God damn. Oof!" He went down like a bag of rocks. Weston watched his team attach handcuffs behind his back and tie his feet with precise moves. Then they stood him on his feet, one holding each arm. Their captive attempted to sway his body away, yet he became unbalanced with each move.

The men ducked and laughed at each attempt at escape and assault aimed in their direction. "We got a live one here, buddy," Agent Harper exclaimed while Adams answered, "Remember that dude in Iraq whose feet we were shooting at," both laughed, adding, "or the idiot on that drug bust who now needs help taking a leak…"

"What about the…" the stalker froze.

Weston glared at him without expression.

"You boys can have him after my chat," he instructed as the room fell silent. "Who are you?" The person turned his head away. One of the men turned his neck to have their captive face forward.

"The boss asked you a question." The other slapped his face.

"It doesn't matter who I am. You are too late." They went to hit him again, but Weston held up his hand to stop.

"Okay, you are right. I don't care who you are. Where is Rina?" The guy stood arms crossed, giving Weston the stare down. "I'm only going to ask you once more, where is Rina?"

"What kind of deal can you give me?"

"Ah, why do they always go for the deal?"

"Unless they are trust-fund kids, then they go for the lawyer, right boss?"

"Sir, you are not in a good bargaining position. You will tell me where Rina is, and then you will have a chat with my boys here about other information that may come in handy. Do you understand?"

"I know my rights. I want my lawyer."

"Trust fund kid," Harper and Adams high-fived, and one collected a couple of bills from the other.

"Fine." The two men dropped him on his butt and then went to help Cowboy stand. Weston took a penlight out of his breast pocket and started to walk towards the exit. The two followed, holding Cowboy by his shoulders and dragging him along.

"Wait. You can't leave me here…" Weston stopped and turned.

"We are leaving you temporarily as we can only help one person out at a time. Don't worry, I'll send back someone to get you in a few hours, and then you can call your lawyer."

"You really can't leave me here. They'll come looking."

"Who are 'they?'" Weston waited for a beat and then turned to leave.

"Wait! Rina is in the warehouse. Please do not leave me here." Two other men stepped out of the darkness. Each took an elbow to help him stand. "You set me up!"

Weston smiled. "I'm just getting you to your lawyer faster." Harper handed Weston a walkie-talkie, which he turned on and held the receiver to his ear.

"They are at the warehouse."

"Do you have any other information?"

"He wants his lawyer." Marty's laughter made Weston smile. "What's our plan?"

"I'll meet you in the garage in ten. We can go over logistics and get your new best friend, a holding cell."

"I'll send down a sweep team. Can we still use this one as a bargaining chip?"

"Possibly, but I think we are better off using Beman. We do have Beman on tape planting evidence on Mary's computer, which connects him, Mary, and Marshall Butman."

"We can use Beman if we can find him. I think he still believes that he is part of your team."

"What do you mean, find Beman? He was taken into custody at my place before we left, wasn't he?"

"About that—"

"Marty, are you kidding me?" Weston's shouts echoed in the tunnel. "We had him and the evidence—"

"We can't use it, though…"

"Yeah but—"

"Look, Wes, everything for a reason, remember? Let's see what else our friend Wayback knows."

"Hey," the captive stopped walking. Weston turned in the direction of his voice. "Mary and Butman are the brains here. I'm just a hired gun and Wayback..."

"What about Wayback?"

"He just got caught up in it all, and we were using him to bait Luna. She wouldn't cooperate with the family business if you know what I mean, and she wanted a hippie lover –"

"Enter Wayback."

"Exactly. She's cute, and men think with their –"

"Okay, we get it."

"Really? Because I don't. Wayback became a total sucker if you know what I mean. And once mama saw the connection well let's just say she strongly suggested--"

"Forced?"

"Yeah, that mama can be bat shit crazy. She wanted the whole family to live in a compound she found, so if Wayback was part of Luna's vision, well, mama was going to make it happen."

"What else did mama want?"

"I don't know grandchildren? All I know is whoever killed Luna will pay. Mama will make certain."

"Get up, you are leaving," Meth Head Biker Dude directed from the doorway. Rina rose and stretched. The stench from her body permeated the area. She discovered why people always say hippies stink.

"Can I use the…" she pointed to the bathroom. Meth Head nodded as Rina closed the door. She washed her face and armpits while watching herself in the mirror. Her eyes were red and swollen, her complexion ash. Hair stuck to the side of her head, and her dress was smeared with grime, "And this is how I am going die," she muttered at her reflection.

Meth Head held the door open. Mary waited in the other room, along with two men Rina did not recognize.

"Rina, these are your new escorts Roach and Rocco Tremont," Mary instructed. "Please don't give them any difficulty." She smiled and turned her attention to the well-armed men. Each had a rifle slung over his arm along with a small gun in a leather holder. Both men wore buzz cuts and had the same spider tattoo Wayback had on his wrist. Theirs appeared across each left bicep. Dressed all in tight black workout pants and t-shirts, they looked like they belonged in a gym, not escorting her to her demise.

"And if she does give you any inconvenience, shoot her," she added with a serene smile. Rina flinched with that last remark. Each man took an elbow and led Rina out of the building. Sunlight temporarily blinded her as strong arms directed her body towards a large vehicle. Cold air encompassed her figure as the ice-cold leather seats produced bumps on her skin.

The vehicle rocked as each took their seat in front. She heard someone speak "ready" as the truck began to move. Rina sat in the middle of the back seat, visible in the rearview mirror for the driver. The tinted windows provided little scenery to see outside. She put her head back to stare at the ceiling and silently began to curse Weston. Somehow she knew this was all his fault.

Weston paced with one hand on his walkie-talkie and the other resting on his gun. The warehouse where Rina was being held had been under surveillance for more than a week. The tracker he installed on Mary's car seemed to lead his team back here regularly. After the day's developments, they observed an increase in activity in the area.

Marty had moved the DEA's part up to this evening. Divers, boats, and other armed forces were already in a position to progress at his or Wes' signal. If the plan worked, the prize, or heroin shipment, along with the brains behind it, would soon be in their custody. Getting the distribution list with all the addresses would make pick up much more straightforward.

Back at their observation point, just to the left of where Wes stood, Beman watched the monitors. Marty thought it would be an excellent move to keep him close and see who else they could tie into this mess.

Weston thought otherwise. Beman's presence made for another distraction he currently didn't need.

"Hey boss, we have movement," Agent Marconi stated as he sat right next to Beman. Marty had filled the room with his team, yet Weston still had trust issues all around. A small cargo ship pulled into one of the boathouses.

"Where?" he asked. With two quick strides, his face leaned in between the two. Marconi pointed to the screen. "Ship is in, and isn't that Mary's car?" A quick nod confirmed.

"There is also an SUV following behind." Weston watched the two vehicles move in unison, each taking the same path. "Looks like they are heading around to where the boat is docked."

Weston brought his walkie-talkie to his lips. "Okay, guys, Team A: take out the SUV on my queue, and be careful. They are carrying precious cargo. Teams B: continue to monitor the first car. See if they make any unusual shifts once their friends are gone. And Team C: whenever you are ready, take out the boat and crew. Try to be as discrete as possible." He leaned back over the monitor.

"Team A up in about three minutes, they will reach the intersection of Main and Dockside. Block the second vehicle there. Team A, stand by." As Weston turned to walk away, he glanced down at Beman. His hands shook, and his face had paled. "You alright, buddy," he asked as he slapped his shoulder, sending Beman's body forward.

"Just a little nauseous," he responded. "Must have been something I ate." Weston nodded and moved towards the door. With a slight head nod, another gentleman followed.

"I want him out of here," he stage-whispered.

"When?"

"As soon as I give the signal for the second team to move into place." The two walked back in and took their places. Weston stood within full view of the entire room, and his counterpart went behind Beman. They watched the first car turn and then, with sheer precision, collide with the second car.

Upon impact, Beman rose. He turned to see his colleague blocking his path.

"Going somewhere?"

Rina's right shoulder hit hard just below the window. "What the…"

"Get her out of the car. She's our ticket out of here!" Rocco opened the door and dragged her out. Shouting came from all sides.

"Hands up and drop the gun—"

"You drop your weapons, or the girl dies." Rina felt a sharp object poking her head. She lifted her arm to shoe it away. Pain shot up her back. "I'll shoot you right now if you don't behave," Rocco said in a stage whisper. "What's it going to be boys? Your boss's girlfriend dies, and you take us in, or you lend us a vehicle and try another day?" Rina hated the crazy person laugh that came out of his mouth.

No one moved. Rina scanned the crowd for Weston. No matter how many times he left her out to dry, Rina couldn't help but think he was going to rescue her.

"Stop crying," Roach stage whispered a bit too loud. "You were supposed to be fish bait, not a hostage."

The two parties watched each other. The SUV's exterior heated in the summer sun, yet no one moved. Rina's shirt stuck to her back while her shoulder ached, and her body shook. She watched a helicopter circle and leave. She could hear cars from a street close by, but nothing else.

Seeing Roach and Rocco draw their weapons made her stomach queasy. She dry heaved hunched over a few times, then one of her captures pulled her back up to standing. *This isn't like in the movies,* she thought. *If it was, they would have shot these two already. I am surrounded by freakin' idiots.*

She watched another car, a duplicate of the rest, pull in behind the line. Her stomach flipped. "Just shoot me now," she whispered.

"We can't. You need to be alive to get us out," Roach said.

"You're an idiot," Rocco responded.

"Am not," the two started to argue while Weston approached what had to be the leader. Rina watched as they spoke for a few minutes. When he looked her way, her stomach flipped again.

Weston said something, and the guns pointed in her direction went down by each man's side. He walked to the front of the lead vehicle and shouted something. Rina waited for the guys holding her to respond.

"You really are an idiot…"

"I did what I was told. How is that being stupid…"

"Because."

"Because you are both idiots," Rina stage whispered between clamped teeth. "That man is trying to talk to you." One squinted while the other hiked up Rina's arm. "Eek," she squeaked.

"Please don't hurt her," Weston stated. He now leaned out in the open against the grill. Arms folded, he waited for a response.

"Give us a car…"

"Can't do that."

"Then, she gets it." Rocco poked the gun against Rina's head. She looked at Weston. He gave a slight upward grin before going back to an expressionless face.

"If I give you a car, you will take her with you. Mary and Marshall have already been picked up. They said that you two put this whole thing together, and you are responsible for the heroin shipment down at the docks. If that is true…"

"Damn it. Those idiots!"

"I can't believe they ratted us out…"

"What do we do?" The person holding Rina slammed his hand against the SUV, leaving a dent. The gun started to shake next to her head. "You want her?"

"Not especially," Weston replied. "She's kind of a pain."

"You got that right." The three men laughed.

"What I would like is to have a conversation similar to the one I had with Mary. Maybe we can strike a bargain?" Weston watched the two turn toward the vehicle. He couldn't hear their whispers. The gun remained focused on Rina.

He watched the shadow move on the backside of the vehicle. With a slight head nod, Weston moved two others to relocate in a side position. All stood in silence. Their hands rested on their weapons. Weston caught Rina's eye again to give a slight nod. To his delight, she answered with a similar movement accompanied by a death stare.

"So, what's it going to be?" Weston asked again. He watched the talker cross his arms and look back at the other guy with a head nod. Weston let out the breath he had been holding in as the shooter dropped his gun.

"We want to see our lawyers," Roach stated while agents swarmed in from all sides.

Rina clasped into one of her liberator's arms. She heard Weston say he would take over as familiar arms circled of warmth around her.

"You okay?" he whispered. She nodded back. Another person handed her a bottle of water, which she proceeded to chug down. Something warm touched her forehead. She looked up into his warm brown eyes and kicked him in the shin. Weston winced.

"That is for dragging me into this mess." Before he could respond, her foot connected with his shin again.

"Ow!"

"And this is for Doc and for Cowboy—" Weston moved out of the way before Rina did any more damage.

"Doc and Cowboy are fine. Look," Weston pointed to the back of a vehicle where Rina could clearly see Cowboy's face. "He's sleeping off a tranquilizer, and Doc will be at the office when we get there." Rina got quiet for a moment.

"Imbecile," she grunted, yet she moved her body to connect to his.

"Yeah, but at least I'm your imbecile…" Rina pulled back and laughed. "I mean, yeah, but I am all yours … You know, you could really use a shower." Rina balled her fingers into a fist, hurled her arm back, and connected with Weston's jaw.

"Ow!" He dragged her tight against his body with one hand, while rubbing his jaw with the other. Weston then leaned in and whispered, "Love is real…" into her ear.

Passenger

LM Pampuro

Acknowledging Those Who Helped Along The Way:

Many assisted in making this story come alive. First and always, I am grateful to my dedicated editor (& niece), Ms. Amanda Pampuro. Without her patience, this couldn't happen.

I would also like to thank my Beta readers: fellow traveler Terri Linea Meigs, playwright extraordinaire MJ Feely, my cohort in academia Stephanie Fischer, my Godfather Bobby Calegari, and the ladies of CoLoNY for their indispensable feedback.

There are always people who breeze into your life and have faith in the work you do. Jamie Cat Callan, Kay Janney, and Chris Archer, you were "those people" for me.

Especially with this book, I need to thank my mom and dad for having the faith to allow me to go off and follow a rock band, yet more important, to know I would come back home.

To my fellow followers, and you know who
you are, thank you for the adventures.
We had good times, good music, and
safe travels.
To Café Sol, for free WiFi and the best milky
Chai Tea around.
Finally, to my rock and roll traveler husband,
let's keep enjoying the adventure!

Also, by L.M. Pampuro,
Dancing with Faith
Maximum Mayhem (Zack & Maxi's 1st adventure)
The Perfect Pitch
Passenger: the only game in town
Uncle Neddy's Funeral
Maximum Trouble
Harlot's grace
Harlot's fire
Visit her at Pampuro.com